IZAR,
THE AMESBURY
ARCHER

IZAR, THE AMESBURY ARCHER

A Pioneer Metal Smith

MICHAEL E WILLS

Also by Michael E Wills

Finn's Fate
Three Kings – One Throne
The Wessex Turncoat
One Decent Thing
A TEFLER's Tale
Children of the Chieftain: Betrayed
Children of the Chieftain: Banished
Children of the Chieftain: Bounty
Children of the Chieftain: Bound for Home
Sven and the Purse of Silver
The Red Slipper

INTRODUCTION

Gaining a true understanding of the distant past is very difficult because all detail about times gone by is judged by a reader, subconsciously, against the standards of morality, the customs, the beliefs and the traditions of the present day. We are, without realising it, prejudiced. The picture we get about historical information is, in our minds, inadvertently influenced by the way we think and act in modern society. To get a better understanding, we must try to put ourselves in the position of those who lived in the relevant period. Yes, it is very difficult, and no period is more difficult to come to terms with than the Stone Age.

Compared with our times, life in the Stone Age was immensely different and to us might seem to be backward and simple. However, it is unlikely that the people who lived then were any less intelligent than we are. The problem is, we know very little about them. Though they did not leave any written account of how life was, they did leave some tantalising, lasting clues. Among these are cave paintings, vast monuments like Stonehenge and carefully laid out burials, all of which give fascinating glimpses into life and times before the use of metal and recorded history.

Apart from the things they did and the way they lived, there is the intriguing question about how they interreacted with each other. The morals and behaviour of our time are largely based on religious teaching of some sort. This is true whether we are believers or not. Did Stone Age people have a moral code of any kind? Did they steal, murder and exploit others with impunity, or were there strict behavioural traditions? I have assumed, perhaps wrongly, that feelings such as sympathy, gratefulness, compassion and aggression, are innate in humans, no matter in what age they lived.

In writing this story, I drew my inspiration from the grave of one man, which was found near to Stonehenge. Intriguingly, scientific research has shown that though he was buried in Wiltshire, England, he was born very far away, in the area of the Alpine mountains. His skeleton and many of his personal possessions are in the Salisbury museum. The exhibit gives a fascinating insight into life 4,500 years ago.

Consider things we regard as basic, which this man might not have been able to do. Counting, for example. We count using a base of ten, a system probably invented in India two and half thousand years ago. So, how would our Stone Age man have counted his goats once he had more animals than he had fingers? And yet, at that time, some people were able to do the intricate mathematics needed to build monumental structures that aligned with the sun and the moon.

How did they make things? There were no metal hammers and nails, so how did they construct places to shelter from wind and rain? The myth that Stone Age people lived in caves could not possibly be true in most cases, as in many parts of the world there are no caves. And did the people have names? It seems to me that they must have had some way of identifying themselves, and not just themselves, but places too.

Another thing that is difficult to appreciate is how very, very slowly technology developed at that time. The technique of making an axe four thousand years ago would probably be almost the same as that two thousand years earlier. Compare this with the lightning speed of technological development in our times. Remember for example, that a hundred and fifty years ago we had no cars, aircraft, radio, telephones or penicillin.

But in the lifetime of the man whose skeleton I referred to earlier, things were about to change; new technology would bring the Stone Age to an end.

Direction of the setting sun in summer
Home of the
Silurian Tribe
Home of the
Dumnonii Tribe
Stonehenge
Home of the Duran Tribe and
Durotrin, (now called Durrington
Walls, near Amesbury)

Direction of the summer rising sun
Old Zef's workshop
Home of the Rhetian Tribe
Direction of the
sun at midday

"Any sufficiently advanced technology is indistinguishable from magic."

Sir Arthur C. Clark.
Inventor, Futurist and Science Fiction Writer

CHAPTER 1

The boy nervously gripped his bow as he peered into the dense fog, the fog which often laid an impenetrable, damp, white blanket over the mountain after the snows had melted. He had made the bow himself from a branch of an ancient yew tree. It was strung with sinew from a deer. The grip on the weapon was slippery with the wetness of the heavy mist. He held an arrow in his other hand, the stone tip, which he had also made himself, pointing to the ground and the feathered flight resting lightly in his hand as he stood prepared to defend himself. He, his father and younger brother were far from their home when the fog had carpeted the mountain. He had panicked and called out to them. His voice had been heard by those who lived nearby. They set loose their dogs to find the trespassing stranger. The animals were barking excitedly but the fog prevented him from seeing them and, fortunately, them from seeing him.

"Can they smell my trail in this weather?" he asked himself. He knew that if they did get his scent, he would have no chance of evading the men looking for him. But he could not run towards the safety of his family's territory, for if he did, he would surely be heard as he scrambled on the loose stones.

The day had been fine when they had set out on their hunt. He could clearly see the long, magnificent mountain chain, much of it still snow clad. They were high above the treeline on the mountain sheltering their distant homestead when the fog began to roll in. His job had been to try to cautiously circle round a herd of deer and drive them towards the others so that they could ambush the animals. He was a long way ahead of them and he knew from the smoke he had seen earlier that he was very close, dangerously close, to the settlement of an unfriendly clan in the tribe the boy belonged to, the Rhetia. While he had never seen them, he knew that they were referred to as the "miners". They were mysterious people who lived on the mountainside. All day their fires burned, sending up so much smoke that it could be seen from a great distance. He did not know why they did this, but he had been warned that they jealously guarded their secret and intruders were very unwelcome. It was also said that the secret gave the leaders of the clan great mystical power.

He was getting cold and wet. How long could he stay still? His legs were beginning to ache. The dogs were getting closer. The damp air played tricks with sound, but they seemed to be above him, further up the slope, to one side. If this were so, they were between him and his family's territory. He must move soon, but he was trapped. The only route to escape was down the mountainside to the forest below. There he could hide up a tree until the searchers gave up.

He slowly lifted his arrow and slid it back into the quiver on his belt. Then he slung his bow over his shoulder. He could see enough of the ground to be sure where the mountain sloped down. He paused, nervously wondering if he was doing the right thing. Then, the renewed barking left him with no doubt. The sound was not the yap of small animals, but the deep-throated intermittent roar of big beasts.

He started to gingerly tiptoe over the mountain scree, trying to avoid making the stones rattle. It was impossible. There was a clink, clink sound as he moved. The barking intensified. It was nearer now. He gave up caution and started to run down the steep slope. As he did so he slipped and slid. Several times he fell painfully onto the unforgiving rock. The barking was getting closer, but the dogs still could not see him, and each time they stopped to sniff for his scent, he gained a little space between them and him. The boy began to be hopeful. He could make it! He could reach the trees. He would be able to find a hiding place!

But he was wrong. Suddenly, even in the bad visibility, he saw with horror that where ahead of him there should have been grey mountainside, there was nothing. It was a cliff edge! He tried to stop, dropping to his bottom with his hands on the ground. Such was his terror of the gap in the ground in front of him he did not notice the pain from the skin of his palms being torn by the sharp stones.

His fall was short, but the impact sent a searing shock through his body. He had landed on his hands and knees on a wide flat rock. His first thought was that the dogs could not follow him over the cliff. For this, he felt relief but nothing else as he submerged into deep unconsciousness.

He was aware of voices long before he opened his eyes. Voices that were arguing. But the hurt he felt obscured his ability to understand what they were saying. He tried to analyse where the throbbing pain was coming from by making small movements, slowly stretching his fingers, then his arms. But the agony was constant, unaffected by him doing this. Then he moved his legs, first one and then the other. He gasped with anguish: the leg on the side where he kept his quiver was the source of the torment.

As he drew a deep breath, the noise of the argument briefly stopped. The speakers had noticed that he had made a sound, that he was conscious. Then the row erupted again, though louder. He opened his eyes and, without moving his head, glanced around him. The fog had cleared. Two men were standing, looking down at him. One of them, the tallest, was dressed in a leather shirt and leggings. Even from where he lay, Izar could see smears of black ash on the man's clothes. In his hand he had a wooden club. The other man was bare legged and wore a long leather shirt open at the front. Around his waist he had a knotted strip of thin rope into which was tucked a long flint knife. In his hand he held an axe, the white stone head of which was raised threateningly. Between Izar and the men, with her back to the injured boy, a woman held up a flint dagger, the point of which was directed towards the man with the axe.

"Leave him, leave him I say!" she shrieked.

"But what good is he, his leg is shattered, he'll never be any use to us!" shouted the axeman.

"Just another mouth to feed. Give him to the dogs," said the other.

"He can be cured; we need workers in the mine."

The woman was almost hysterical now and prodded the axeman's bare, sooty chest with the end of her knife. As she did so, an old man, dressed in a similar fashion to the axeman, shuffled into view from around a rocky outcrop. He was carrying a spear, which he pointed towards the two men.

"Do as your mother says, move away, let me look at the lad."

The two assailants glanced at each other, then scowled at their father before taking a step back. The old man put the wooden end of his spear on the ground and used it to prop himself up as he leant forward to examine the boy. He prodded the leg causing most of the boy's pain and looked to see his reaction. It was instantaneous: the prone body went rigid as the boy screwed up his face and gasped.

"Can you do anything with his leg, woman?" he said, looking up at her.

"It'll take some time, but he's a strong looking lad. He'll live to work for you."

"How old is he?"

The woman leant forward and picked up one of the stranger's hands and spat on the back of it. She used her shawl to wipe off the blood loosened by her spittle. She was looking for the tattooed spots that all people had on the base of their fingers. Each summer a new spot of ink was ingrained with a bone needle, at the base of a different finger. When all the fingers had been marked on both hands, a second row was started above the first. No one ever lived to have more than four rows.

"That one is full, let's see the other," she said.

She repeated the slimy process.

"That one too and four more dots marked as well. This boy will be a man soon."

The father stood up, turned to his sons, and growled, "We give the boy until the leaves fall, to be walking. Then he can work."

The man with the club said with disdain, "And if he doesn't walk?"

"Then we put him into the forest for the wolves to take care of."

"You are too soft, old man. Your mind is getting weak. We don't need the likes of him here," said the axeman.

"Not too soft to put my spear through you. As long as I breathe, I lead this clan, you will do as I say or you will be cursed and cast out of the village. If your women folk produced children who lived to this boy's age, we wouldn't need to look for labour."

What the old man had said stung the two brothers. The fact that all their children had died at childbirth or soon after was a constant lament from the prospective grandfather. The younger men realised that there was no point in arguing further and turned to walk away.

"Come back, Riker, you and Nir take the boy to our hut."

They turned back and begrudgingly put their weapons down and bent to lift the boy. It was obvious that they were being vindictive when they roughly hoisted him up.

"Not that leg, you fool, Riker. Put your arm under his thigh," instructed the woman. "Do you have a name, boy?" she asked.

"Izar," he answered between gasps as the two heavy-handed men lifted him.

The woman walked alongside them and said, "And where have you come from?"

"The other side of the mountain, my family keep goats."

Riker scoffed and said, "An ignorant peasant, what use are you to us?

"Hold your tongue, Riker," she commanded.

"My father is an arrow maker too," added the boy.

"Did he make the ones in your quiver?" asked Nir as he grabbed the quiver and pulled one out.

"No, I did."

Both men looked at the arrow and, while secretly admiring the workmanship, did not comment further.

The place where he was taken was one of many simple huts around a flat, though rocky, open space. The men crouched to get through the low door and in the gloom inside, with no thought for his physical state, dumped Izar on a pile of furs. The only light in the hut came from the dying flames of a fire on a stone hearth in the centre of the room.

The men left and their place was taken by the old woman.

"Bring wood," she called to the men.

"Now, Izar, we have to see what you have done to your leg. When the fire is brighter it will become clearer. But first I must wash the blood away."

He tried to sit up, supporting himself by putting his arms behind him with his palms on the ground, but quickly abandoned the position when the pain from his torn hands briefly competed with that from his knee. Instead he raised himself as much as he could by resting on his elbows behind him. He saw that the woman had brought a bowl of water into the hut. She sat on the ground by his feet, cutting up softened leather with her knife.

"Wood, bring some wood I said," she shouted.

The light coming through the doorway was soon dimmed by the figure of Riker carrying a bundle of kindling. He put some thin logs onto the fire and blew at the embers to encourage the flames. Then, without saying a word, he left.

The woman leant forward and, as she did so, he noticed that she wore a necklace – a leather thong on which were some highly coloured beads, probably made from baked clay and painted. This betokened that she was a woman of some status. Gazing at the injured leg, she said, "We must get you closer to the fire so that I can see if the leg can be saved."

She pulled at his uninjured leg to twist the lower part of the boy's body nearer to the light.

"I have to cut off your leggings, they are torn anyway."

Izar leant as far forward as he could manage, to watch. As he did so, he saw for the first time the mess of blood-soaked leather legging that had been ripped by the impact. The red fluid had not yet congealed and indeed he could see that fresh blood was leaking from the position of the wound. Despite the gruesome sight and the prospect of worse pain when the woman started to investigate the injury, something distracted him. The knife the woman was using to cut up his legging was not the one she had had earlier when she threatened the axeman, Nir. The blade she was now using was glinting in the firelight. It flashed and reflected light as she used it. He did not know, but though it was not as sharp as a flint knife, she believed that it might have mystical power to help her to carry out the intricate task before her.

"What manner of stone is your knife, woman?" croaked Izar.

She leant forward and whispered, "In due course, when your wound has recovered, if you find favour with my man, you might find out."

Izar saw no more as the pull of the knife on his leggings multiplied his pain and he collapsed backwards, and once more he slipped into unconsciousness.

CHAPTER 2

"Here, drink this," said a woman's voice. "Lift his head up, Riker."

Izar opened his eyes and focused on the face in front of him. It was that of an old woman. Her grey, straggly, shoulder-length hair hung forward as she leant towards him. On seeing her, the memory of what had happened to him re-emerged.

"Drink this for the pain, boy."

She held the clay beaker to his lips, and he sipped the potion. It was warm, but bitter. He was aware that there were lumps of some kind floating in the liquid.

"That's good, chew on the bark in the drink. Willow helps to dull your ache."

She had described it well: the pain was now not so much a piercing one, but much more of a throbbing ache.

Izar strained to look down at his knee in the flickering light of the fire. There was nothing to be seen apart from a bundle of soft leather wrapped round the middle of his leg, tied on with animal sinew.

"Ha, see, you still have two legs, you young whelp," growled a man's voice from behind him, from where an arm also stretched forward to support him.

"Most parts of them!" said another man's voice.

The two men laughed.

"And here is what is missing!" exclaimed Riker.

He held a small clay dish in front of Izar. On it were some shards of bone in a pool of blood.

"Take it away, be off with you. Stop scaring the lad!," shouted the woman.

Riker let go of Izar's head abruptly and it fell back, hitting the fur-covered floor. There was a silence, then his weak voice asked, "What's happened to me?"

"Your knee was smashed to pieces. I had to take the broken bits of bone out or they would have killed you."

"Will I die anyway?" asked the boy feebly.

"That depends on how strong you are."

The woman paused and thought of the time limit she had been given to heal her patient.

"The spirits will test you, for you are certain to have a fever. They will decide whether you have the will to live."

"But can I ever walk again?

"If you survive the fever, you will eventually walk again."

Izar smiled, closed his eyes and fell into a fitful sleep.

In the future, Izar would never be able to describe the terrible torment of the fever, for he would not remember. Those around him had a more vivid impression of the cruel tribulations that the spirits imposed on the boy as he lay twisting and turning, screaming and crying, sometimes shivering, other times throwing off the fur that covered him, streaming with sweat. His fever lasted for two days. During that period the old lady sat with him for much of the time. More than once, when it seemed the boy might succumb to the spirit of death, she chanted to beg a supernatural power for help. She bathed his forehead when he sweated and covered him over when he shivered.

"Why do you waste your time on the boy, Mother? If he lives, he will be a burden to us. He will eat out of our cooking pot, but never put anything into it," growled Nir.

"The best thing would be to smother him now, before he wearies you more," added Riker.

He picked up a wolf's fur and lifted it to cover the boy's head. The woman picked up her knife, the one Izar had seen glinting in the light and pointed it at her son.

"Begone, be off with you. Leave the boy in peace. Go back to work."

Riker threw the fur down on the ground and made for the doorway with his brother. He turned and shouted, "You heard what father said, this pup has to be working before the leaves fall from the trees. If he doesn't then I will tear him limb from limb and feed him to the dogs."

It was not long after their departure that the injured boy started to mumble. At first the sounds made no sense, but then quite suddenly, he murmured, "What is this place? Where?"

He tried to raise his head to look around the gloomy hut but gave up.

"So, the spirits have allowed you to live. That is, at least until the end of the warm season."

It was clear that the boy was recovering his memory of what had happened, for he suddenly raised his head and threw off the fur, straining to look at his leg.

"What has happened? What did you do?" he asked desperately.

"I did what had to be done. Are you hungry?"

He ignored her question and in a pleading voice asked, "Can you make me walk again? Do you have the power?"

"You alone hold the secret of your recovery. You must learn to walk with a stick and then, when you are strong enough, you may manage without help."

The woman did not want to repeat the time limit that had been set for him to begin to contribute to the small community.

They both gazed at the blood-soaked leather dressing around his knee, and then she added, "You have survived the fever, now you must start to use your leg before it withers."

"Withers?"

"If you don't use the leg, you'll lose the use of it." She paused and then added, "I'll warm the stew, you can eat and then rest, but after the next sunrise you must start to walk."

She lifted the clay pot and placed it on the fire. When the mixture of herbs and meat was warm enough, she passed it to Izar. Supporting himself on one elbow, he dipped his hand into the warm contents of the pot and felt around inside until he found a piece of bone. As he gnawed meat from the bone, she left him and went outside.

When no light came through the smoke hole in the roof, Izar realised that night was falling. This was confirmed when the old woman and her man came into the hut. As they had pushed aside the skins that hung in the doorway to hinder the cold air coming in, there was no glimpse of light. They sat down on furs by the fire. The man stoked it and threw a log on, then the woman put the pot of stew back on the fire. Izar was offered no food, for he had already eaten.

"The boy can share our hut for a few days until he gets stronger," said the woman.

"You are a kind fool, Stin, but I fear you are wasting your time."

"He's strong and might recover."

"Remember, woman, he must be useful to us before the cold time, our boys won't accept a parasite living here."

Izar felt very uneasy on hearing the man's comment, but decided it was best to pretend to be asleep. As he lay on his fur, despite the argument going on between the two of them, he turned his thoughts to wondering if his father had been out searching for him. It was likely that his family would assume he had been eaten by wolves.

In the morning, the man left the hut as soon as light started to penetrate the smoke hole. His woman, who Izar had realised was called Stin, busied about in the hut tidying and arranging the fireplace, ready to light the fire. She took her fire bow and twisted a hard, straight stick in a loop in the bowstring. One end of the stick was placed down into a hollow in a block of wood, which was covered in finely cut wood shavings. She held the stick upright and supported the top with one hand. With the other hand she pushed the bow back and forth, level with the ground. After a while the heat from the bottom of the stick rubbing against the softer wood caused a little smoke to rise. As she worked with the bow, she sang a chant asking the fire god to make flames. Suddenly, there was a small red glow in the wood shavings. She blew on them and they began to burn. Soon the whole pile was alight. Stin shook the burning wood into the hearth and piled sticks on top to build the fire.

While she was heating up the cooking pot, Izar raised himself to a sitting position. He was conscious of the pain in his injured leg, but it was not as bad as yesterday.

"We'll eat first. My man, Rab, will come for food before he starts to work. Then we'll begin to make your leg recover from the injury. What did you say your name was boy?

"Izar."

"Take this then, Izar, and scoop up some food from inside," she said as she passed him the clay cooking pot.

When Rab came in, he had in his hand a thick stave.

"You're going to need this," he said gruffly to Izar. As he spoke, he threw the stick onto the ground beside the boy.

And so, after they had eaten, Stin helped Izar to his feet and the exercising began. Although she had been caring before, she now showed no sympathy for the boy as he winced with pain when he tried to move around the hut, supporting himself with the stick.

"Stop whimpering, you must learn to overcome the pain. Unless you can then there is no future for you."

Izar understood from the comments he had heard the day before, that she meant what she said. He had to persevere, though it might take a long time for him to recover.

On the third day of his recovery, Izar ventured outside the hut. His eyes, which had been used to the gloom inside, were dazzled by the sunlight. But he did not need his eyes to tell him that there were dogs nearby. It was the same sound that had driven him down the mountain. He immediately recoiled and turned to go back into the hut.

Stin, who was just emerging through the doorway, pushed Izar gently and said, "Turn back, don't worry, the dogs are tethered."

Izar slowly made his way past another hut and there, behind it, were four large, grey dogs tied to a line that allowed them to run a short distance in any direction. All four of the dogs strained the leather straps holding them as they tried to reach the stranger. They barked loudly and snarled at the newcomer. Izar stopped.

"I told you, they are tethered," shouted Stin with annoyance in her voice.

"Why do you keep them here?" asked Izar.

"Why do you think, you young fool?"

"I mean so close to the huts."

"As you hear, no stranger can get near without us knowing, and at night they are let loose to guard us."

"You have enemies?" asked the boy.

"There are those who would like to take power from us. But the dogs have another use too," she said slowly.

"What?"

"They stop some people leaving here, those who we would wish to stay."

Stin was silent for a moment and then said, "You have too little to do, you must make yourself useful any way you can. You can take over my job of caring for the dogs."

The prospect did not appeal to Izar. He asked cautiously, "What must I do?"

"They are fed in the morning and again in the evening. The people in the valley bring us meat for the dogs when they bring our food. This evening I'll show you what to do."

And so began Izar's job as dog keeper. At first, he just threw the meat towards the animals for them to pick up. His limited mobility prevented him from making sure that each dog got a fair share. As the days passed, he took more interest in each of them and dared to approach them to share out the bones and offal the villagers brought.

While the dogs got more friendly, the two brothers got less so. They became even more cruel and made fun of his disability when they met him. Izar was always nervous when they passed. They looked quite sinister. Their faces were often covered in soot, as were their arms and legs.

"Here, Izar, lean on me," said Nir.

Izar was puzzled by the offer. Riker took the stave and Izar leaned on Nir as he walked.

"Now try by yourself," instructed Nir, pushing Izar's hand off his shoulder.

Izar stood wobbling on one leg.

"Give me my stick, Riker. Please, give it to me!" pleaded Izar.

"Get it yourself," said his tormentor as he threw it into the undergrowth.

The two brothers laughed and continued on their way as Izar collapsed to the ground and then started to crawl to retrieve his support.

The scene had been witnessed by a young boy, the son of one of the villagers. Izar had noticed him before; he had a withered left arm. His hand was in place, but he could not use it.

Apart from when he shyly glanced up to watch Izar's plight, the boy stood still, his eyes looking at the ground.

Then, without saying a word, he walked ahead of Izar, over to the undergrowth, and pulled the stick out from under a bush.

He went back and passed the stave to Izar, who had stopped crawling and was now sitting, waiting.

"Thanks. I could have got it myself but…."

As Izar's voice trailed off, the boy cautiously said, "It was easier for me."

Izar did not like to admit to anyone that he was handicapped, even less so to this young lad. His thanks to the boy were less than effusive, a fact he instantly regretted. He asked the boy to sit down on the dusty ground beside him.

"Why are you not working like the other children?" asked Izar.

The boy held up his deformed arm.

There was a long, awkward silence, which was eventually broken by the boy, who nervously said, "You look after the dogs, don't you?"

"Well, yes, I am learning to know them."

He seemed to be gaining confidence when he said, "And they are learning to know you. It will take time; they are very angry with strangers."

Izar thought for a while about what had brought him here and caused him to have the fall.

"Yes, this is true. What's your name?"

The boy looked sadly at the ground as he said, "Lin, but the other children call me 'Cripple'."

"Then I'll call you Lin. How old are you?"

Lin raised his right hand for Izar to see the spots on each finger and then, with his right hand, he raised his other arm. One finger had a spot.

"Lin, can you help me to stand up? If I push with my stick and lean on you, I should be able to do so."

Lin once more averted looking at Izar's eyes and said, "If I help you, will you be my friend?"

Izar suddenly felt ashamed of himself. He was injured, but had hope of making some kind of recovery; this boy had no chance of a normal childhood in the rough world of village life, where he was obviously already singled out as one to be ridiculed. How would his adulthood be? And yet, Izar had not really thanked him for his help in retrieving the stave.

"Yes, of course I will. If you get me one of the fire logs outside the house over there, I'll make something for you. Get one of the shorter ones. I need some rocks too. Come with me to help me find the kind I want."

And so, despite their disparate ages, began a friendship between the two. Lin was frequently bullied by the other children and while Izar could do little to prevent this, he was able to offer consolation to the boy when he came weeping to him. Izar found it strange that Lin preferred to find solace with him and not with his parents.

However, their association was positive for Izar too. It led to a rekindling of his interest in using skills his father had taught him. These included fashioning flint blades, and a talent he had developed at his father's knee – wood carving. Within days, Lin was the proud owner of a carving of the head of one of the dogs.

From comments he had heard between the family members, Izar had understood that the brothers worked in some fire pits on the side of the mountain a little way from the settlement. They were not alone, for there were other men who lived in the village who also worked there breaking rocks. Every day, men came up from the valley, bringing wood from the forest. From a distance, Izar had seen that they lit great brush fires against the mountainside. They piled logs onto the burning brush and the fires burned all night. In the mornings they threw water onto the hot rock. As the steam cleared, he saw that the stone was split. What they did with the split rock he could not see, though he was intrigued to find out. But for now, it was impossible for him to walk over the uneven path to where the work was taking place.

As the warm season approached and the days lengthened, Izar's walks did too. He usually took one of the dogs with him for company as he spent longer and longer hobbling around, regaining some use of his injured leg. Gradually, he was able to bend it a little, and the leg was getting noticeably stronger. Eventually, he made his way to the quarry to watch as the men, sweating in the sun, beat the split stones with rocks to pulverise them. Rab often walked among them, shouting orders and selecting which stones should be beaten into even smaller pieces. When he was satisfied that the bits were small enough, he scooped them into a sack.

Izar still had too much time on his hands and needed to occupy himself. He watched with envy the young people in the village running and jumping in play and undertaking the many physical tasks required of them by their parents. Often Lin was amongst them, but usually unable to do what the others were. Izar too felt left out and regretted that he could not offer to work for the good of the village. A strong need was developing within him to find something useful that he could do despite his physical limitations. He needed to gain the respect of others; he increasingly felt that he was regarded as of no worth to the community and no better than a beggar. The answer came to him while he was watching the miners adding to the heaps of discarded rocks around the quarry. He decided to collect some of the rejected stones and use the skills his father had taught him to make arrowheads.

He made his choice of stones by tapping them with another rock to see how easily they would flake. When he had found a few that might be suitable, he took them back the hut. To work the stone, he needed to first make some tools from the antler of a red deer. In a corner of the village there was a pile of dry bone refuse and there he found what he was looking for. He borrowed a stone axe from Stin and cut off several sections of an antler to make pointed tools of different sizes and one thick piece about the length of his hand. He then spent hours sitting on a boulder outside the hut with the stone he had chosen to work on. He placed it on a piece of leather on his good knee and held it with one hand, while he patiently used the various tools to remove small flakes. Even with extreme care, it took many attempts to prevent the finely worked flint from breaking, but eventually he succeeded in making two arrowheads.

"See, the boy is some use to us," said Stin as she handed the two finely shaped arrowheads to Rab.

"He'll need to do more than this if he is to justify all the food he eats," the man replied with irritation in his voice.

Without much enthusiasm at first, he stood examining the arrowheads, one at a time. He knew that it was important for the arrowhead to be well balanced with the same weight of stone on each face, for if it was not, the arrow would not fly straight. Clearly Rab was impressed. He said, "He uses his hands well. I saw that he has also carved on wood some fine images of the dogs, too."

"He gives them to the village children. He first made a flint blade to cut the wood," answered Stin with some pride.

Rab was quiet for a while and then said, "Has he seen your knife?"

"Only very briefly, when I was picking the bone fragments from his knee. I'd thought he was unconscious."

"Be careful, woman, he might ask questions. We must protect our knowledge. It's best that only you and our sons know of the existence of the knife."

"We have to learn how we can copy it. When we have done so, we can stop trading our copper with the men who come from where the sun rises, and use the metal to make things ourselves."

Rab stood scratching his beard, his face contorted as he considered carefully what he was going to say.

"What is it, Rab? What are you thinking?"

The old man hesitated and then said, "We might make knives more quickly if we did share our knowledge with the boy."

Stin looked at her man quizzically for a few moments and then exclaimed, "To make the casts?"

"Yes, my hands are too old, and our sons have no ability to work with delicate things."

CHAPTER 3

Riker was kneeling by the side of a round, clay-lined indentation on the ground. It was filled with burning charcoal. His father and brother were standing, bending to watch the progress of the fire. There was a small hole in the ground outside the fire pit; it was the opening to a short tunnel, the other end of which was inside the circle.

Rab watched while Riker, covered in soot and sweat, directed the opening of the blowing bag into the hole. The bag was made from deer skins. Several were sewn together to form a round container. Inside were some bent branches; their springiness held the bag open. As Riker forced the bag as flat as he could, air was pushed out in a narrow stream through the hole and onto the base of the fire. When the pressured air hit the glowing charcoal, it flared intensely. As he relaxed the pressure, the bag re-filled with air.

"Faster, Riker, faster, the stone will soon melt," instructed Rab. "Nir, get more fuel."

Nir reached as closely as he could into the fire and dropped more charcoal onto the inferno.

Earlier in the afternoon, Rab had carefully placed on top of the unlit fire some of the crushed rocks he had selected at the quarry. From his experience he knew that the green stone contained traces of the precious material. Earlier, men from the village worked at the ovens to roast this crushed stone, though at a lower temperature. But Rab and his sons kept to themselves the secret of getting the stone to change into copper. Only they worked on the second burning in this, the hottest fire they could make. And it was this closely guarded secret that gave them their power and position.

"Leave this fire now and let's see what we got from yesterday's," ordered Rab.

The men walked a short way to where there was another fireplace. The fire had gone out and there remained just a heap of grey ashes.

Nir put his hand onto the heap and said, "It's cooled down. Riker, give me the rake."

Riker passed Nir a stick on which was tied a short piece of a deer antler. Dust rose and covered Nir's arms as he pulled the ashes from the hollow in which the fire had burnt. As he got deeper, he worked more slowly until he came across something hard.

"Let's see what we have got," said Rab impatiently.

He leant over and peered into the embers as Nir raked out an uneven, gnarled, brownish-yellow lump.

Looking up at Rab, he said, "It's good, but too hot. Riker, get water."

Riker slowly poured water into what remained of the grey ash and dowsed the metal. While it was not shiny, it did have a dull lustre.

"Give it to me," ordered Rab.

Nir carefully lifted the small, lumpy shape, water dripping off as he did so, and passed it to Rab. The old man wiped the little clump of copper on his leather shirt and then held it up, inspecting it carefully.

"A good day's work, but we need more, much more. Nir, prepare this place for a new fire and, Riker, go back to the other one and blow more air to keep it hot."

Izar had often seen the smoke, but he did not know what they were burning or why. The fires were some distance away, too far for him to venture yet.

Nevertheless, he kept busy. When he was not exercising, he often continued making arrowheads and carving the images of the dogs from lumps of wood. He persuaded Stin to give him back the bow he had the day he fell from the mountain. He had made a polished stone wrist guard to protect his arm from the bow string and spent hours occupying himself by practising his archery skills. There were several poles outside the huts that were used for hanging dead animals on when they were being gutted. He used these poles as targets. This gave a double benefit as he not only improved his archery skills but also got plenty of exercise in retrieving the arrows, sometimes from the poles, but most often from the undergrowth beyond.

It was in this undergrowth that Stin had her beehives. Several trees had been cut down, leaving stumps half the height of a man. These had been hollowed out, a hole cut in from the side for the bees to enter and the tops covered by flat stones. Twice Izar had seen Stin and two of the forester women, with cloths over their heads for protection, lift the lids and harvest the honey. They also kept the beeswax, which they used for making candles.

The boy was surprised and pleased when Rab started taking an interest in the things he was making. The old man had begun stopping to watch as Izar used his stone blade to carve wood. He was flattered by Rab's attention and although he would not have been capable of analysing these feelings, Izar was subconsciously aware that any appreciation of his efforts made him feel of more value as a person.

One day, the old man asked, "Can you carve anything you want?"

"No, only things I have seen, like dogs or deer."

"So if I show you something, you could make its likeness?"

"I can try," answered the boy.

Rab sniffed and said, "Can you?"

When he had left, the two brothers appeared. Nir grabbed the bow that was propped up on the side of the boulder and took an arrow from Izar's quiver. The boy was very anxious that the bow should not be broken. His anxiety turned to anger when the man pulled the string back a few times. Back much further than would normally be necessary to fire an arrow.

"Please, please be careful. It might break!" Izar exclaimed.

"That would be sad, Izar, wouldn't it?"

Riker laughed and seized the bow. He tugged at the arrow in the other man's hand.

"Let's see how good the bow is. Give me the arrow, Nir. Give it to me!"

There was a crack as the arrow shaft broke.

Izar could not contain his anger. He pushed himself up with his walking stick and then raised it over his head.

"Be gone, be gone. Leave me alone or I'll crack your skulls!"

Neither man took the threat seriously until Izar brought the stick down onto Riker's shoulder.

"Why, you little rat," said Riker as he raised his fist.

"Stop, stop! Let the boy alone. Be about your work, the two of you."

Rab had heard the shouting and hurried back to the boulder where Izar usually sat.

Riker glowered at Izar and slowly lowered his fist. The boy was relieved that the two brothers obeyed their father.

"Get back to the charcoal oven. We'll need some fuel. The men have brought more wood up from the forest."

Resentfully, the brothers turned and started to walk back towards their workplace, but not before Riker had spat on the ground in front of Izar and made a gesture with his fist.

When they were out of earshot, Rab said in a quiet voice, "Be careful, my sons have foul tempers and they don't forgive those who cross them."

"Thanks for your help. What is the charcoal oven?"

Rab hesitated and fumbled for an answer. The question seemed to have changed his mood, for eventually he answered in a sharp tone, "No business of yours, boy."

He turned and followed the brothers towards the place of the fires. Izar picked up the two halves of the broken arrow and considered if it would be possible to repair it or whether he should salvage the feathered flight, which he had carefully glued onto the shaft with birch root resin, and the stone tip to make a new arrow.

It was at about this time that Izar moved out of the old people's hut into a dilapidated shack that had belonged to Rab's parents. Unlike most huts in the village, his was made of hazel branches interwoven through a framework of birch poles that formed a dome. Rab had helped him to replace some of the branches, and Stin stitched patches on the holes in the weather-beaten leather sheet, which covered the frame to keep the inside dry. She had given him some fur mats to use as a bed. The door opening was blocked by a hurdle to keep out the goats, and over it hung a deer skin to protect against the wind and cold.

When Izar had moved his few belongings into the hut. Stin said, "It is the custom that when a man moves to his own house, he should have his own drinking beaker."

She returned later carrying a clay pot.

"Here take this one, it was my mother's. We should have buried it with her, but she had another from her mother."

The boy was moved. It was a mark of friendship and respect to be given a beaker for his own personal use. At his home he had to share one with his brother and would not have had his own until he was a man. The valuable beakers were made far away by skilful potters using clay that could not be found in this region. They had to be bought by trading them for things like stone weapons, woven blankets or animal skins.

Izar often gazed at the beaker, studying its shape and the patterns on it. It had a wide middle and a narrow top. The decorations showed the sun on each side. On one side the sun was low over a line, which was the horizon. On the other side it showed a high sun. He began to wonder if he could copy these pictures. They were too delicate to carve on wood. He needed some other smoother surface, but what?

Although he now had his own hut, he still joined the old couple at mealtimes, and the bond between them continued to grow, much to the annoyance of the two brothers. However, while Stin was invariably friendly and caring, Rab was less so.

One day when they were eating together, Stin said, "You will need the beaker in a few days, for the sun will soon reach the highest point of the year. Rab will decide when the time is right."

When the chosen day arrived, the deep sound of someone blowing a ram's horn woke the boy; it was just getting light. He knew what this meant: it was today which, according to Rab, the sun would be at its highest. The day to thank the spirit of the warm season. When Izar drew back the hurdle and the deerskin curtain at the entrance to his hut, he saw in the half-light that a lot of people had already gathered outside. The foresters, the poor folk who lived in the valley and supplied wood for the fires, had joined the miners and their womenfolk to watch the sun rise.

Outside of the hut belonging to Rab and Stin was a log covered by a woven cloth. The skins over the entrance to the hut parted and Rab came out, followed by Stin, each with a beaker in hand. Then they stood side by side watching as the glow intensified, betokening the rise of the sun. The old man leaned forward and pulled the cloth off the log. It was hollowed out and the void filled with a yellowish fluid, fermented honey. He dipped his beaker into the liquid and then Stin did so too. In order of status, others queued to do the same. First Nir, the older brother, then Riker. Next, the miners, though many did not have a beaker of their own and approached the log in pairs or threes. Finally, the foresters who also shared their beakers. When all the older people had scooped their drink, Stin beckoned Izar to fill his pot. She then started chanting, and other women joined in. It was a repetitive tune that lasted until the first ray of sun broke out over the forest below. Everyone turned to look at Rab.

"The sun reaches its zenith today as it did for our father and our father's fathers and those before. We give thanks for the warm time and pray for a good harvest and the return of a new, young sun after the cold and darkness of the frozen time to come."

He held his beaker up as high as he could reach, and the crowd did the same. They all turned to the sun and drank of the liquid. Then Rab filled his beaker again. He walked over to the beehives and slowly poured the contents onto the ground around them. He incanted, "Oh, Spirit of the earth and mountain, all good things come from you, I return to you some of your own."

Izar watched the ceremony, aware of people's belief that the spirits of the earth and the mountain must be repaid for providing the things people took from them. He had seen this too when the miners refilled the holes they made once they had extracted what was needed. The damage to the land had to be repaired and recompense made to maintain the favour of the spirit of the mountain.

As the sun rose, those in the gathering began to disappear and return to their daily tasks. Izar was about to go into his hut to bring out his bow when Stin called to him.

"Come, this is the time to mark your hand, and ours."

She went into her hut and came out carrying a basket. She put it onto the boulder on which Izar usually sat.

"Rab, your mark first." He walked over to where she stood and held out his hands."

Izar could see that there were three complete rows of black dots on his two hands, and in the fourth row just two fingers had no mark. He was indeed an old man, his life almost spent. The boy wondered if old Rab would share his secrets with others before he was laid in his grave.

Stin used a small, flat piece of wood to stir the gall from an oak apple with water to make a black fluid. She dipped a bone needle into the ink, took hold of the one of Rab's hands that had the spaces and pierced the skin of a finger with the needle.

Each of the brothers came forward, and finally it was Izar's turn. When it was done, he wiped the blood and the excess ink on his sleeve, grabbed his stave and went to feed the dogs.

CHAPTER 4

Izar had begun to think more about his own father and mother. Soon his leg would be well enough for him to leave this place and attempt to walk to the other side of the mountain, where he had lived before. But he also faced a dilemma. He was beginning to feel at home in the mine workers' settlement. Stin was now like a second mother, while Rab was reasonably friendly to him and seemed to have some respect, even admiration for what he could do. And the mystery of what was happening here was now intriguing the boy to the point of fascination, though no one would tell him anything about it. The problem was the two brothers, who seemed to dislike him even more now than they did on that terrible day when he first met them. They bullied him, mocked him and did everything possible to irritate him.

One evening, soon after the longest day ceremony, after the fires had gone out and Izar had fed the dogs and gone to bed, Nir and Riker appeared outside of their parents' hut. They were obviously expected, as Rab came out followed by Stin. He pointed to a place by the stream that ran down from the mountain, the place where the villagers got their water. Rab cautiously looked round to make sure that they were alone and then beckoned the brothers and Stin to sit on the ground.

"Very soon the traders from the Noricum tribe who come from where the sun rises, will come to do business with us. We must decide what we should do," said Rab.

"We must get beakers, bowls, cloth and other things to give to the forest people, for they provide our food, and we grow nothing here on the side of the barren mountain," answered Nir.

Nir was referring to the fact that, in their community, the foresters provided not only wood for their fires, but also farm produce and game. In return, Rab and his family supplied them with things they could not make, hunt or grow. These were obtained by trading with the Noricum.

"Yes, it is the understanding we have among our people. They provide for us and we for them. But we could give them more if we had copper knives and spear heads to trade with other settlements," interjected Stin.

Riker protested, "Remember, the traders have warned us many times that their master alone has the privilege from the spirit of the earth to use the copper."

"I believe we can have this right too," said Stin.

"Ah, Mother, you dream as usual. Yes, we can make the fires hot enough to melt the copper, but we have never tried to mould the metal. We would need to make casts to form it. We have never done this," said Nir.

Before Stin could reply, Rab broke in. "I have an idea. We could make the moulds, the casts, with wood."

"Wood?" exclaimed Riker.

"Yes, wood," answered Rab.

"But the molten copper would burn the wood," argued Riker.

"Not if we put a thin layer of clay on the mould."

"Rab is right, we should try it. Think what high status and good trade we would have if we could use our copper in this way," said Stin.

Nir spoke with enthusiasm, "It's true, Riker, it would give the people in our clan more wealth and we would have even higher status among the Rhetian people."

"If we did this then we would have nothing to give the traders this year and we would starve," said Riker.

Rab answered quickly, "You are right, Riker. But we will offer them half of the copper we have made this year and keep the rest. This way we can still trade with them."

There was a long silence that was eventually broken by Nir.

"So, we must make a wooden mould, how should we do this?"

"Have you seen the work the boy has done? He is very skilful with his hands. I am certain he could make moulds for us."

"The brat?"

"Riker, he is called Izar," said Stin angrily.

"But he would learn our secrets. Only we know how to make the charcoal that gives enough heat to burn the rocks, and only we can make the stones give up copper. This knowledge has been passed from your father to you and his father to him for generations," growled Riker.

"Yes, and to make a mould you would have to show him the knife you traded last time the Noricum came. It is too valuable for a stranger's eyes," added Nir.

"I am afraid he has already seen it, though he was delirious and has perhaps forgotten," said Stin.

Rab struggled to get on his feet and then looked down on the others as he spoke. "It is necessary for him to see the knife if he is to make a mould, for if we can make others like it, our family will win great respect. I have decided."

The others looked up at the old man in silence.

Nir was first to react. "So be it, but we will watch the boy closely, and if he betrays his loyalty to us, his death will follow."

Riker quickly said, "At my hand."

Stin was last to speak and she said slowly, "You have decided well, Rab. So be it."

"After we have eaten our morning food tomorrow sunrise, I will tell him what he is to do," said Rab. "Come, Nir, Riker, we have work to do. We must hide half of our copper, for the traders will not believe that we have so little to trade with them."

Riker groaned. "We are making a mistake. You will regret this, old man, and you too, Nir. Mother, your head has been turned by your affection for the brat."

"You either do as I command or leave the settlement," hissed Rab.

Riker was silent. Despite his growing fury, he was aware that they would never allow him to leave; he knew too much about what happened here. If he tried to leave, he was sure they would kill him to protect the secrets that gave the family its status.

Next day, when Izar went into Rab's hut for morning meal he had an uneasy feeling that there was some tension. Rab was not conversing as loudly as usual, and Stin seemed to be watching him closely.

"When you can walk without a stick, will you want to leave here?" asked Rab abruptly.

Izar was surprised by the question and stumbled for an answer. Eventually, hesitantly, he said, "You have looked after me well and my life is good here, though your sons do not want me to be part of your family."

"So, will you leave?" asked Stin.

"First I must repay you in some way by working. I could help with the fires."

"If you work with us, if we make you one of our family, you will learn how by burning rock, you can have status. By sharing our secret, you will gain knowledge that few have. Knowledge gives power."

"You mean that, that you will teach me? That I will learn the ways of the miners?" Izar stuttered.

"Yes and much more. But there is a trade and a test," said Rab.

"A trade?"

"You trade your life for our trust. For, once you have the power that comes with this knowledge, you may never leave here."

Izar was silent, trying to take in what had been said.

"Why do you hesitate?" asked Stin

"I, I fear your sons, and they will hate me more if I stay too long."

Rab laughed and said, "You have nothing to fear, as soon as they realise how important you are to our future, they will respect you."

"You said that there is a test?"

"Yes, you must first show me that you can be of value to us," said Rab.

"What should I do?"

Rab looked at Stin and nodded. She went to a corner of the hut, while Rab put more wood on the fire and blew at the embers to get more light.

Sitting down beside Izar, she held out the knife and said, "This is what we want to copy, using our own copper."

Izar gazed at the implement, moving his head to look at it from different angles.

"It's a knife?"

"Yes, but not made from stone."

"But how could you make it?"

Rab had been silent longer than usual, but could contain himself no more. "We have not made it. We traded it for copper that we produced here. It was made by a craftsman from a distant place in the direction of the rising sun."

Izar took the knife from Stin and examined the cutting edge and the balance of the implement. He held it up so it reflected the light of the flames.

"It's beautiful. Can we really make such a thing?"

"I believe that we can. Do you want to help?" asked Rab.

"Yes, yes very much. What should I do?"

"I want you to make the shape of this knife in wood, two pieces of wood. It must be very exact. Can you do this?"

"How do you mean? I don't understand."

Rab was exasperated and threw his hands up to demonstrate his feeling.

"Rab, you are too impatient, let me explain," said Stin.

"You try then," he said, resigning himself to the fact that his wife might do better.

Stin reached across and grabbed a piece of bread from the clay dish containing their morning food.

"Look, Izar, if I push the knife flat, hard into the bread, and then you remove it, you'll see what happens."

The boy leaned forward and took the knife out.

"You see the shape left in the bread? It is a perfect copy of the shape of the knife."

"Yes, of course."

"We want to make a perfect copy of the knife in wood."

Izar hesitated and then said, "But wood is harder than bread."

"Yes, so we want you to cut the wood very carefully to make it the same form as the knife. This will be in two halves, one for one side of the knife and one for the other. Can you do this?"

"Well, yes perhaps, but I think it will be difficult. I'll have to scoop out the shape from a flat piece of wood. After cutting, I should rub the surface with sand to make the shape as smooth as the knife."

"Good, then you should start today. Now we shall eat."

Stin offered Izar the piece of bread with the indentation of the knife.

CHAPTER 5

Izar's sense of inferiority because of his physical handicap was not helped by the cruelty of some villagers. They laughed at his awkward way of walking and often called him names. His ability to carve wooden figures and make arrowheads had gained him some little respect, but not with everyone. Now, he realised that Rab's offer could give him the chance to be equal, no, even superior to most of the villagers. No longer would they look down on him. There would be no more taunts. But first he must prove himself in the eyes of Rab and his family.

It was no easy task to make the wooden mould. First, Nir had to use his stone axe to cut some short logs from one of the branches the forest people brought up the mountain. Then he had to split the log as exactly as possible, down the middle. The knotty nature of the wood made it quite difficult to get a smooth split. All of Izar's work had to be done in secret as previously, only Rab and his family had ever been allowed to see the knife.

"Try these two halves, Izar," said Nir as he handed a split log to the boy.

He carefully measured the log against the length of the copper knife.

"The length is good but the grain in the wood is not straight, it will be difficult to carve with the detail needed."

Nir shook his head and said, "It's taking too much time to do this, but I'll try to find a better log."

While Nir searched for the right kind of timber, Izar continued with the making of the stone knife blades he would need to do the carving.

The situation was now very strange. Earlier, Izar had been treated badly by the brothers and shown no respect. Now, Nir was forced to be more reasonable to the young one who might hold the key to an improvement in the status of the family.

While Nir had been working with the wood, they had seen little of Riker. He had been away at the fire pits for most of the time. When he did appear, he scowled at the process of wood carving and the people involved in it.

"These are the best ones," said Izar as he inspected the two halves of a log Nir had given him.

"How long will it take make the mould? asked Rab, peering over Izar's shoulder.

"I don't know, for I must work slowly," replied Izar.

The mould took a very long time indeed. Try as he might, Izar found it extremely difficult to cut out the shape of the copper knife accurately. Nir was forced to supply more logs as the boy failed several times in his attempts to make the shape. After three days of meticulous work, Izar called Rab to look at his best effort to scoop out the wood to the right shape.

"This is the best I can do, the knife fits into the two halves very closely," said Izar.

Rab inspected the carved shape and placed the knife into one half and closed the other half on top.

"Um…near enough, but it has taken too long."

Nir was watching and said, "Yes, it's near enough, we can try the mould to see if the process will work."

Rab stood holding the log mould, staring down at it. Then he turned to Nir and said, "Yes, we'll try tomorrow. Tell Riker to prepare charcoal to heat the copper."

The old man took the knife out of the mould, looked at Izar and gave him the two halves, saying, "Cut a channel at the tip of the handle for us to pour the molten copper in."

"Can I watch you do the work tomorrow?" asked Izar.

The two men looked at each other and then Rab said, "No, not this time. If the process works then you shall help next time."

Izar spent the next day in nervous anticipation, wondering if his work would prove to be useful to the family. It was late in the afternoon when the two brothers and Rab appeared in the village. Izar saw them coming and limped over to meet them. He was immediately concerned to see that they were not smiling.

Riker was arguing loudly.

"I said it was a foolish venture. A waste of time and now the whelp has some knowledge of our work."

"It might work if we could protect the wood from the heat," replied Nir.

Rab saw Izar and beckoned for him to join them by the boulder where they usually talked. When they got there, he held up the two pieces of Izar's beautifully carved mould. It was charred black and the shape of the knife was unrecognisable.

"But, but did you make a knife?" stuttered Izar.

Rab held up his hand. In it was a piece of copper with a shape recognisable as a knife but with ragged edges and a distorted blade.

They all looked at the misshapen implement.

"Izar, the good thing with this copper is that we never waste it. Not like when you make an arrowhead, how many do you break before you make a good one?"

"More than the spots on one hand," he replied.

"Exactly, and each one you break is wasted. We can take this knife and melt the copper to create a better one."

"I say it is not worth trying again, the wood burns even with a clay coating," moaned Riker.

"What do you think, Nir?" asked Rab.

"If the coating is too thick, the mould will lose its shape. We could try again, but if it takes another three days to make a mould this is going to be a very slow process. We must have a new mould for each cast of copper."

"Wait, wait," stammered Izar.

"Quiet, boy, we didn't ask you to speak," retorted Riker.

"No, please listen."

"What have you to say, Izar?" said Rab.

"Don't waste your time listening to rubbish from him. Let's give up the idea and return to producing and trading copper, just as before," growled Riker.

"No, listen to what the lad has to say," interjected Nir.

There was a short silence punctuated only by snorts of indignation by Riker.

"Please, you said that if the clay coating is too thick, the mould would lose its shape."

Nir and Rab nodded their heads.

"But what if the clay was the mould?"

"How do you mean, boy?" asked Rab.

Izar held out one hand with the inside upwards.

"If we take a flat piece of damp clay and press your copper knife into it, like this," he explained, motioning by pushing his other hand into the first, "we will have the exact shape of the knife."

"And then what?" scoffed Riker.

"And then the molten stone, the copper, can be poured into the clay mould. It would take the shape of the knife."

"Show me what you mean," demanded Rab.

Somewhat hesitantly, Izar said, "Could you get me a piece of bread and one of my arrows?"

"Bread, arrows, why do you put up with this madness!" shouted Riker.

"Shut up, Riker. Nir, go to the hut and get some bread. Pick up Izar's quiver when you come back."

Rab, Riker and Izar waited by the boulder in an awkward silence. When Nir came back, Stin was following him. "I want to see this idea the boy has," she said.

Izar smiled and quipped, "Well it is not really my idea, but yours. You did this with the knife."

He took the lump of soft bread and pressed the flat side of arrowhead into it.

"Now if the bread had been clay, we would have a perfect copy of the arrowhead that we could pour copper into. When the metal cools, we would have a copper arrowhead."

There was a long silence while Stin and the men thought about Izar's idea.

Eventually, Riker started laughing and said, "That can't work. The copper is heavy, it would cause the damp clay to lose its shape."

Rab held up his hand and said, "What Riker says is true. But we could overcome this difficulty if we let the clay dry hard before using the mould."

Riker was not to be satisfied, for he laughed again and then said, "But don't you fools see, if you did this, you would have the shape of one side of the arrowhead but the other side, the top of the copper in the mould, would be flat."

There was another long silence, eventually broken by Izar.

"Then we could make two moulds in clay."

"How do you mean, boy?" asked Nir.

"To make a copy of the knife, first, you make a clay cast of one side, then a second cast of the other side."

"And then?"

"If the two moulds are put together, bound tightly, the molten stone can be poured into a hole in the cast. This way the copper would have two sides, just like your knife."

Rab smiled and said, "Izar, this is a good idea, but just as the clay we have in the river in the valley is not good for making beakers, it might not be good to make moulds."

"But let's try, Father. It would be much quicker than using wood," urged Nir.

From that time on, despite the rantings of Riker, Izar was deeply involved in the testing of the new way to make the copper casts. Although Rab had had misgivings, the clay from the river served their purpose well. But the method did not immediately work exactly as Izar had predicted. At first, the moulds cracked when the copper was poured in, but eventually Izar realised that the mould had to be heated before filling. After many attempts, each one improving on the last, they succeeded in making an accurate copy of the original knife.

"You see there, Riker, it is possible!" goaded Rab.

"You have wasted many days to make one knife when we could have been producing copper to trade with."

"The time was not wasted, Riker, it was necessary to find the best method," said Nir.

Unwisely, Izar commented, "We have gained much knowledge of making casts. I am sure we can do even better next time."

If Riker was merely irritated before, he was now furious.

"Do you allow this mis-shaped brat to tell us what is good or bad!? Is he the one who decides for us, are you too old and feeble to be the wise one any longer?"

"Hold your tongue and respect your father!" shouted Nir.

As Riker raised his fist to hit his brother, Rab stepped between them, shouting, "Enough, Riker, enough!"

Riker paused, then slowly lowered his arm. He turned and looked straight at Izar, saying, "You are a curse on this family. Before you dropped from the mountain, all was well here. Now we are divided and no good will come of it."

As Riker stomped off in the direction of the village, Rab called after him, "I may be old, I may be feeble, but I am not afraid of new knowledge. If you resist new ways, you have no future here."

There was a long silence, which was eventually broken by Izar.

"The surface of the knife is not as smooth as it should be. I will try to improve this by rubbing first with sand and then with coarse fur."

"Good. Take the new knife to the village and do it secretly in your hut. When it is finished, I will call the villagers together, show them the knife and tell them how it is a token of good things for them in the future," said Rab.

Izar wrapped the knife in a piece of soft leather and did as instructed. Later, away from prying eyes, he did all he could to perfect the surface of the metal. He spent many hours rubbing sand on the blade to remove the slight imperfections and also to sharpen it. Finally, he polished the metal to get the best shine possible.

When Rab was satisfied with Izar's work, he called the villagers to come to listen to him. Standing in front of the tall poles Izar used for targets, the old man raised his voice as loudly as he could.

"For many generations my family has produced copper from the rocks that you have mined and broken up. My forefathers passed the secret of the alchemy to me. Every year we trade our copper with the men from where the sun rises for the things we need, the things we cannot produce ourselves. The trade has been good, but now it can be better. We are going to trade with other Rhetian villages ourselves."

"Why would they need the copper?" shouted one man. Several others mumbled in agreement.

"We will not be trading raw copper; we will trade copper goods!"

Rab turned to Izar, who was unwrapping the leather. He passed the knife to Rab, who held it aloft.

"This is what we can now make ourselves, from our own copper."

There was a gasp from the crowd and they surged forward to inspect the object. Despite the fact that many of the villagers had been involved in the process of producing copper, none of them had seen it used. Rab passed the knife to a man in front of him. He looked carefully at the knife and then passed it to another, and he to another, though some did not dare touch the extraordinary substance.

"See what new knowledge and ability we have? Such knives will bring our village great fame and status, and trading them will make us more secure."

There was no doubt about the villagers' enthusiasm, but Rab and Stin knew that there was a fundamental challenge, and that was the wrath of the Noricum.

Nevertheless, production of the knives started and they very slowly began to build up a small stock of them to use for future trading. Several of the women in the village worked to make the bone handles into which the tang of the knives where inserted. They were affixed with a stronger glue than that which Izar had used for his arrows. The women mixed pine tree sap, ground charcoal and beeswax to form a sticky mass, which hardened to be like black stone.

It was when Izar was polishing the blade of one of the knives that he got his idea. An idea that held the possibility of leading to his reputation being elevated even higher. As he rubbed the copper, he recalled the pattern on his beaker, a pattern he could not carve in detail because the surface of the wood was too rough. The copper was smooth, and if it could be etched carefully with a small, sharp flint, it might be possible to draw a design on it. But the area of surface on a knife was small. He needed something bigger.

"Rab, you once told me that unlike stone, copper is never wasted. It can always be re-used by melting again."

"Yes, this is true. Why do you ask?"

"I would like to try an idea I have, if it does not work then you can melt the copper again." said Izar.

Rab was very happy with the way things were. They had overcome many difficulties and now managed to make at least one knife a week to add to their stock. He had little appetite for any changes.

"We don't need new ideas, the process we use is good."

"But I would like to make something different from a knife, something that might be easier to make and could give you great wealth."

As Izar was speaking, Stin appeared.

"What is this new thing of which you speak, Izar?" she asked.

"You, like many of the women in the village, have small, coloured beads on a leather thong round your neck," he said, pointing at the necklace she wore.

"This is true, and the more beads a woman has, the higher her status," she answered.

"And you also believe that the ownership of copper will bestow great status on a man or woman."

"This is true, Izar, that is of course why we are producing the knives," commented Rab with some irritation in his voice.

"Then, if we made something from copper that people could wear, it would show even more status than the very best beads," said Izar triumphantly.

There was a silence while man and wife considered Izar's idea. Afraid that they were not convinced, Izar spoke again.

"If we could cast copper discs, I could engrave a design on the copper, a picture of the sun, perhaps."

Somewhat begrudgingly, Rab said, "It would not be very difficult to make a disc, easier than making a knife, I think."

"Then let the boy try his idea, Rab," urged Stin.

"We will make two more knives and then try to make a disc such as the boy wants," he replied.

But this plan was not realised, for a very unexpected reason. Two days later in the middle of a hot afternoon, the barking of the dogs, animals that Izar now regarded as his own, announced the coming of strangers – the traders were toiling up the steep slope from the valley.

Izar had heard talk in the village of the traders. They were men who came from far away in the direction of the rising sun and while they were keen to do business, they were said to be very aggressive in dictating the terms of trade. The villagers were much in awe and almost in fear of them.

Izar, who had been practising with his bow, stood by his hut encouraging the dogs to relax as he watched some of the villagers rushing to obey the command shouted by one of the traders to go help them. They were needed to assist in pushing a heavy cart with solid wooden wheels made from slices of logs. Although it was pulled by two donkeys, they could not manage the last part of the steep incline into the village.

The five traders carried bows, and three of them had stone axes hanging from their belts. Rab held up his hand in greeting, and one of the men, who seemed to be the leader, responded likewise. They obviously knew each other.

Nevertheless, there were no smiles and they both seemed tense. Izar was worried, for he knew that Rab would not be able to supply them with much copper, as the family had saved half of their production for their own secret use.

Some women busied about building up the cooking fire so that food could be prepared for the visitors after business had been concluded. Meanwhile, the newcomers brought the cart into the centre of the village and untied the leather harness on the donkeys, leaving them to graze together with several others that belonged to the villagers. Izar was still standing by his hut, watching what was happening.

"Now let's see what you have to offer us!" roared the leader of the visitors. "We have beakers, bowls and cloth to trade for your copper."

"It has not been a good year, we have less to trade than usual," replied Rab loudly so that onlookers could hear.

"That is bad news indeed, for my master expects me to return with plentiful copper for the use of his men. He alone has the gift from the spirits of the sun and earth to use the copper."

"Nir, get the sack from my hut," ordered Rab.

There was an anxious wait for Nir to return. When he did, he placed the sack on the ground in front of the traders and stood facing them, waiting for their reaction.

"Is there not more!?" shouted the leader.

"As I said, this has been a bad year," repeated Rab.

"You mean I have dragged our cart all the way up this hill to collect just this?"

"Come, have a drink of honey mead and discuss trade with me," replied Rab.

"There won't be much to discuss, but the mead we will have."

He grabbed the sack, looked inside and picked up some of the clumps of raw copper.

"At least the quality is good," he mumbled.

Stin, who had left the group, appeared with a large pot and a beaker.

"Come, come sit on the log and drink some honey mead," she said as she placed the pot on the ground.

The beaker was filled and passed around the group of visitors and the men of the family. Gradually the tension eased a little, but the leader was still grumpy. He looked across to where the brothers were sitting and said loudly for all to hear, "Riker, you are lazy. Why have you not produced more copper this year?"

The brother stood up and raised his fist at the questioner.

"I have worked as hard as anyone and produced as much as ever!" he shouted.

The conversation stopped.

"Where is it then?" asked the leader.

Riker hesitated, swaying in front of them, and then pointed at Rab.

"Ask him!"

"Sit down and shut up, Riker," shouted Nir as he stood up to push Riker back to his place on the log.

"What does he mean, Rab?" asked the visitor.

"The fool is confused by the drink. Go back to your hut, Riker."

"You are the fool, we had good trade with these men before you decided to try the brat's new ideas," growled Riker as he pointed his finger at his father.

"What new ideas?" asked the leader.

Riker wagged his hand at the old man and looked around the expectant faces of the visitors.

"He thinks he can become the new master by using the copper himself!" exclaimed Riker, his voice slurred by the drink.

The leader stood up, slid his axe from his belt and raised it in the air.

"You, Rab, you are cheating me and offending my master. For that there is only one punishment."

CHAPTER 6

As the stone axe was about to descend onto Rab's head, there was a thud. Izar's arrow had hit the leader on the shoulder. His shriek of pain was followed by shouts of horror from the other men, and heads turned in the direction the arrow must have come from. The source was clearly identifiable as the bowman put his weapon down. Three of the traders quickly got up and began to run towards Izar. This was too much for the dogs, who had been sitting anxiously observing the newcomers. As the men came forward, the beasts leaped up, tails erect, snarling at the approaching men. Meanwhile, Izar limped as fast as he could to get away. When, after a few seconds he turned to see what was happening, he realised that there was no way men would get past the attacking dogs. Many of the villagers had also appeared, armed with axes and spears to defend Rab.

The traders were now heavily outnumbered and had fled to their cart.

"Leave them, let them go!" shouted a furious Rab.

"You have made a bad mistake, Rab. The master will not forgive you," gasped the leader, wincing as one of his men drew out the arrow. "I want that boy killed and his head on a pole. Now!"

"I decide who is executed here!" shouted Rab defiantly.

The leader realised that, outnumbered as he was, he could not force the issue. He shouted, "Get the donkeys, we are leaving." Turning to Rab as he mopped the blood from his wound with his sleeve, he said in a menacing voice, "We will be back, this will not be forgiven and if you don't kill the boy, I will."

Rab glared back at the man and waved his hand, dismissing his threat and adding, "You were lucky that he had no force behind the arrow, for otherwise we would have had your head."

The villagers stood by threateningly as the traders hitched up the donkeys to their cart and then carefully started their descent of the hill. As they did so, a man pushed through the crowd and ran off to join the departing traders. Riker had realised that he was in less danger with them than he was staying in the village.

"This has ended badly," said Nir to his parents. "Very badly, for they will be back and there will be many more of them."

"It will take them weeks to get to their master, it is a very long way. They will not be back before the warm time after the snows."

"If we are to make peace with them, then we must first kill the boy," answered Nir.

Rab, who had now calmed down, thought for a moment and then said, "Yes, it must be done, but he can be useful to us for many more sunrises before we need to do so."

Stin was listening to the conversation but said nothing for some time. When she broke her silence, she commented,

"Soon, we will not need to do trade with these men, we can trade our own knives in the settlements in the great forest."

"But the men will come here anyway, and we must have peace with them. So you know what has to be done," said Rab.

"Izar has saved your life. Will you let him be killed!?" she exclaimed.

"It will be necessary," replied Rab.

Izar was too far away to hear the conversation between the family, but it was soon relayed to him by some of the villagers. It was curious and confusing for him to have saved Rab's life, knowing that the same man was going to kill him before the next warm time.

Among the villagers, Izar saw Lin. Tears were running down his face when he stepped forward and confronted him.

"It is not good that you must die," he said.

"No, I thought I was doing a good thing."

"But you have many months yet to live, you can carve more figures."

"Be gone, go away," shouted a woman's voice.

The young boy saw Stin and scampered off. Izar had noticed how Lin was treated with disdain by others, particularly by adults, even his own parents.

"It was a waste of good food to let that boy live. Usually, babies with deformity are left in the forest for the wolves," she said.

"But you let me live and I am deformed," Izar pointed out.

"True, but I saw that you could be of some use to us eventually. The cripple will never be of use to anyone."

"And now that I am of use, Rab wants me dead."

"I heard Lin say that you have many months left, much can happen in that time. Go, feed your dogs, for without them, you would have been dead by now."

After the incident with the traders, work continued as before. Izar's idea to make something other than knives from the copper was forgotten by everyone but him. He dared not remind Rab and risk irritating him. When the snows came, the smoke from the great fires stopped. There was still much work to be done to smooth and polish the produce of the clay casts, and as time passed Izar became more skilful at doing so. He also became more mobile as his leg gained strength, but it was now obvious that he would never again be able to run and would often need the support of a stick. However, gradually, Izar was becoming more and more determined that he would make up for his physical deficiency by increasing his prowess in the mystical skill of making beautiful objects in copper. That is, if his life was long enough.

The passing of time and the constant work slowly eased the boy's anxiety about his decided fate at the hands of Rab. But as the snows began to melt and the days got longer, Izar's concern returned. When would the execution be? How would it be done? He considered trying to get away from the village, but he knew that he could not get far from pursuers at the speed he could walk. And if he did escape, what fate would await him? Starvation in the forest? Death by the jaws of the wolves or the claws of a bear?

Soon the fires were started again and Izar spent time watching and learning. He had realised that when Rab sorted the broken stones, he was looking for some indication to show which ones might be useful.

"How do you know which to throw away?" Izar asked Rab.

"You'll learn, you have to look for the green tinge on the rocks," he answered.

But Rab's interest in teaching the boy this and other skills had diminished. He realised that it was a waste of his time. The boy would not live long enough to use the knowledge. Izar sensed this reasoning too, and also noticed that the once friendly Rab was avoiding becoming too attached to him; he was now offhand and grumpy. The time must be coming when the old man had to do what was necessary to heal the relationship with the traders.

Izar began to get very nervous every time he saw Rab, and this developed into him avoiding the old man. Nevertheless, there was still work to be done and so, occasionally, they spent time together. At such times Izar's fascination with the processes to produce the metal overcame his fear of the inevitable. Rab knew that Izar would never live to share their secrets with others, so he allowed him to watch the making of charcoal, the roasting of the crushed rocks and magical extraction of the copper.

One day, just after the fire of the smelter had died down, Izar said to Rab, "You always add the crushed rock to the fire and then later have to seek the copper amongst the ashes."

"Yes, this is the way it is done."

"Would it not be better to put the rock into a container, a clay bowl for example?"

"How would that be better?"

"Well, you would be able to see the rock as the alchemy changes it and control the heat."

"But a clay bowl would crack."

"Not if it is heated slowly and carefully before it is used in the smelting. You would also be able to see how much copper you have made and would not need to wait until the ashes have cooled."

"I will give it some thought, but Nir will need to be convinced."

After several unsuccessful attempts, Izar perfected the production of a clay crucible. Nir and Rab were soon persuaded and as a consequence, copper production increased.

The time when the shoots on the trees grew into green leaves passed. The hot time came and with it the celebration of highest sun. The miners and foresters joined the family for the ritual pronouncement of the prayer for a new, young sun after the long, frozen time.

Now, Izar had two rows of black spots on one hand, and one row and one single one on the other.

"The boy has become a man, Rab," said Stin when they were alone together.

"The lad will never be a man, his time to meet the spirits is coming."

"When will you do it?" she asked.

"The traders will be here before long so it must be soon. Nir will help me."

"But we are many in the village, we can defend ourselves. Izar is useful to us, we must keep him."

"The master who lives in the direction of the rising sun will send more men to see that the score is satisfied."

"But the boy saved you from having your skull crushed, and, in any case, we can't hide that we are using some of our copper to do what is forbidden by the master."

"Be silent, woman, I have decided."

CHAPTER 7

The sun had not yet risen enough to wake the cockerels in the village when Izar was startled into consciousness by the noise of the hurdle being opened and the drape in his doorway lifted. He recoiled as he remembered that his life was to be the price paid to make peace with the traders.

But it was a woman's voice he heard.

"Izar, put clothes on silently and quickly."

"But, Stin, what is to happen?"

"Today is to be the day for you to die," she whispered. "There is a donkey tied to a tree by the beehives. One of the dogs is also there."

"But, but what should I do?"

"Walk the donkey quietly out of the village and down the hill, then mount it to escape. Quickly."

"You will suffer for helping me."

"No, Rab will think that you have escaped alone."

Izar was effusive in his thanks as he scrambled to put on his clothes.

"Here is some food for you," she said as she passed him a heavy cloth bag.

There was too little light in the hut for Izar to see into the bag as it was pushed towards him.

"Be careful, there is also something useful for you in it. Now hurry, take your bow and the arrows, go!"

"Will not Rab find out?"

"No, he is snoring in his bed furs still. Remember, at the bottom of the hill you must travel with your back to the sunrise, otherwise you may meet the traders. Go, find where the sun sets, there the traders will not trace you."

Stin quickly left the hut, soon followed by Izar. As he crossed the open space in the middle of the village in the early morning light, he was alarmed to see that there were three children playing with a small dog.

One shouted, "Izar is going hunting! Can we come too?" Others joined in.

Two more children appeared to see what was happening. Izar limped past the children and smiled at them but said nothing. He was terrified that their parents might come out to see what the children were shouting about. He strained to walk as fast as he could to cross the village and find the donkey.

There it was, tied up as Stina had said. He untied the leather rope and started to pull the unwilling animal to turn its head. With his other hand he loosened the grey dog, one that knew him well. It was jumping up on him, showing its pleasure to have his company. The children stood behind him watching, then one came forward and helped to pull the donkey. The boy could only use one hand. It was Lin.

At last the stubborn donkey took a slow pace forward, then another and another until it broke into an unenthusiastic walk to the path leading down the mountain. The dog trailed behind, as did four children.

"Go home, go home," whispered Izar to the group of followers. Nevertheless, they continued to accompany him until they could no longer see their huts. Concerned by the unfamiliarity of their surroundings, first one, then two more turned and made their way back to the village. Lin continued and after a short while joined Izar by the donkey's head. He held on to the older boy, steadying him as he started down the precipitous slope. The incline was terrifying for Izar, and it quickly became clear that without Lin's help he would not be able to continue.

The donkey too was concerned about the path down the mountain, knowing from experience the danger presented by the steepness of the track. As it made a slow, sure-footed descent, Izar put one arm around the animal's neck and the other over Lin's shoulders. The dog had no difficulty with the incline and frequently raced ahead, rejoicing in the unusual freedom it was enjoying.

As they reached the lower part of the mountain and the area where forest had been cleared to provide fuel for the miners' hungry fires, Izar could see the smoke from the foresters' huts between him and the rising sun. He was quite exhausted; he had not walked this far since the disastrous foggy day on the mountain all that time ago. He pulled the donkey to a halt.

"Lin, you must go home now. I'm going on a long journey."

"I want to go with you on the long journey."

"No, your mother will be angry."

"She will be glad that I have gone."

Izar realised that there probably was some truth in what the boy said. Lin's tormented face and his continued pleading made it difficult to refuse him.

"You can walk with me for a while, then you must return to the village."

While Izar's legs were weak, all the physical work he had been doing had strengthened his upper body and arms. So, while Lin held the animal still, Izar grasped the donkey's mane and pulled himself onto its back. However, though he kicked with his heels, the animal stayed sullenly motionless. He kicked again, this time harder. Still no movement. He was beginning to panic. He must travel more quickly. When Rab discovered his escape, he might decide to chase him.

It was first when the dog started to bark impatiently at the donkey that it decided to move and then began a slow, even plod with its shadow and that of the rider, and Lin, ahead of them. They followed a path created by the foresters when they had dragged the felled trees towards the mountain.

As Izar leaned from side to side, moving to the rhythm of the reluctant donkey's slow steps, he began to wonder where he was going. "Go find where the sun sets," Stin had said. Lin seemed to show no such worry and dutifully followed his older friend. Earlier, Izar's only concern was to escape and distance himself from Rab and the possible arrival of the traders. Now, he was not sure where he was or where the path would lead them. Would his direction of travel take him near to where his parents lived? Perhaps he could find their hut. But for the moment he had to follow the rough path as it led in the direction he had been told to take. Occasionally, he stopped for a short while to give the donkey a rest and let it graze. He took comfort from the fact that Lin smiled happily when their eyes met, and although the boy was much younger and had no conversation, Izar was glad to have his company. The lad was obviously reveling in the adventure that had unexpectedly relieved him of the drudgery of his normal tasks. However, it was beginning to dawn on Izar that as well as his growing concern about his own welfare, he had an extra and unwelcome responsibility for the younger one.

It was late in the morning, with the sun now almost overhead, when they came to a wide, fast flowing river. It was tumbling down the mountain, fed by the last of the snow melt.

Despite the fact that he did have some human company, Izar had started to talk to the dog and the donkey.

"What do we do now, donkey?"

The donkey answered in its own way by pulling Izar forcibly to the water´s edge. The animal was clearly very thirsty, for it took a long drink before shaking its head, turning and starting to graze. The dog too had a long drink. Izar lay on his stomach on the riverbank and scooped up water into his mouth. Lin did likewise.

"We've had no food, have we, Lin?"

The boy grinned and pointed at the bag Izar had slung over his shoulder. He took it off and opened it. Inside, among other things, there was a birch bark tub with a lid. He prised it open and found it contained sticky honey. He dipped his finger in several times and licked off the sweet fluid. He offered some to Lin and the dog looked on longingly.

"Here, dog, lick my finger," he said.

Izar offered the animal the honey. It sniffed but was clearly not inclined to taste it. Izar rummaged in the bag and found a leather package containing lumps of cooked meat. He and Lin sat on a large boulder and, after throwing the dog a piece, shared one of the lumps.

Delving more deeply into the bag, he felt something hard and cold to the touch. He immediately recognized the shape. It was one of the copper knives! He pulled it out to look at it. It was one he had recently polished, and it shone in the midday sun. Looking more deeply in the bag, he found a second knife.

Izar was totally confused. He knew how precious these implements were to the family. Why had Stin given him two of them? Then he remembered something Stin had said to him that morning, "Be careful, there is also something useful for you in the bag." He now realized what she had meant.

After resting for a while, Izar realized that they were losing time. If they were being hunted, they must move on. He stood up to consider how they could continue their journey. The tree-lined track they had been following stopped at the river, but it was clear from the gap in the trees and the worn grass that it continued on the other side. The problem was how to get across this fast-flowing torrent that presented such an obstacle to a traveller at this time of year. There were two alternatives to continuing in the same direction. The boys were at a place where paths met. In addition to the track they were following, two narrow trails ran alongside the river, one downwards and one up the incline. But neither would fulfill the advice he had been given, to keep the rising sun at his back. He studied the river: it did not seem to be very deep, as he could see stones and rocks on the riverbed. Here and there the water broke over large rocks and left a white trail; in other places the surface was smooth.

Izar decided to wade in a little way to test the depth, and Lin did likewise. Both grimaced as the cold mountain water penetrated their leggings. When the water reached his knees and Lin's thighs, they stopped, and the current swirled round their legs. The dog stood at the water's edge barking and showing no enthusiasm to follow them.

"The day is warm, we can easily dry off if our clothes get wet," said Izar.

Lin grinned and nodded but said nothing.

"Let's try to cross, it must be possible," Izar said to himself more than to his quiet companion.

The little boy nodded unquestioningly. They both went back to where they had tied the donkey to a tree and led the animal to the riverbank. The dog followed them to the edge.

Izar put his bag on his shoulder and took hold of the donkey, shortening its leading rope to help keep his balance. Lin grabbed the other side of its halter. Together they started to pull the animal into the river. After a few steps it stopped and resisted strongly.

"Wait, Izar, I'll slap its backside," shouted Lin, his shrill voice trying to compete with the babble of the rushing water.

Lin let go of the rope halter and started to wade back towards the riverbank on the downstream side of the animal. Izar lost sight of him behind the donkey. Then he heard the scream, a high pitched shriek he would never forget.

The donkey, panicking either from fear of the river or the sound of the scream, kicked at Izar as it reversed towards the bank, out of the rushing water. Izar momentarily caught sight of Lin as he was swept downstream by the current, before he himself lost his balance. He stumbled and fell into the cold river. Izar clung desperately to the donkey's leading rope and as the animal hurried to the shore it dragged Izar with it.

When he reached dry land he was desperate, there was nothing he could do to reach his little friend who was being dragged quickly away from him by the turbulent water. It tore at his heart that he could still hear, in the distance, Lin's screams. But they soon stopped. Izar knew that the small boy would never have survived the cold water and the relentless collisions with rocks as the wild river dragged him away. The donkey started grazing as if nothing had happened. Izar let go of the rope and lay on the path, gasping for air.

All this time the dog had been sitting watching on the grass. It had made no attempt to cross the river. It was as if it knew that the boys were courting disaster. It walked over to the recumbent figure and licked his face. It was not only water it was licking off, but also tears.

CHAPTER 8

Izar spent some time lying on the heather at the side of the path, drying himself in the sunshine. He was haunted by the memory of Lin's screams as the turbulent water dragged the little figure to his death. He felt great anguish and regret that he had not insisted the boy return home when he had finished helping with the mountain path descent. When he closed his eyes, he could still see the cheerful little lad's smile of delight when they discovered the food Stin had packed. Lin had paid an awful price for the excitement of accompanying him.

Izar's despair was heightened when his mind turned to his own present situation. He realised that he was trapped. He could not go back for fear of a dreadful reprisal and his way forward was blocked.

Eventually, the effort of the journey and the heat of the sun caused him to submerge into a fitful sleep.

It was the sound of voices that brought him back to reality. He was instantly alert. Pulling himself up, he looked back along the trail he had travelled to see if he had been followed. It was deserted, but the voices were getting louder. He quickly realised that they seemed to be coming from the row of willow trees along the forest path leading up hill, beside the river.

Very soon, two men emerged from the cover of the hanging branches. They were walking one behind the other with a pole between them, which was resting on their shoulders. Strung upside down on the pole was a small deer, its head in death, hanging down and blood dripping from its mouth. The hunters had their bows slung over their backs.

"Greetings," said one of them, raising the hand not steadying the pole.

"Greetings, hunters, I see you have had good luck," answered Izar nervously.

"Good hunting skill, boy, good skill."

As they got closer, the dog started to bark menacingly, and the donkey raised its head to spectate. Izar quickly put the two knives deep into the quiver on his belt.

The men stopped by the riverside and lifted the pole off their shoulders, placing the deer on the ground. One of them waded into the water a few paces, then turned and shouted to his companion as he retraced his steps.

"We can get across here, but it will be very difficult to carry the deer."

The other man turned to Izar and, looking at him in a threatening fashion, said, "We need to use your donkey."

It was obvious that he had no choice but to agree. Restraining the dog with one hand, he picked up the donkey's leading rein, which was dangling in the grass, and handed it to the man. He was very worried, for if the hunters stole the animal, it would be impossible for him to continue his flight.

At the same time, it seemed that these men knew a safe way to cross the river, which he could use.

Izar walked across the grass to help the men untie the deer from the pole and then held the donkey still while they placed the dead animal across the donkey's back.

"Are you coming across too?" asked the man who had been in the water.

"Yes, I am travelling towards the setting sun."

"Come with us then, the dog will swim."

The man already in the water grabbed the rein and pulled the frightened animal towards the river. the other slapped the donkey's rump with the flat of his hand, while holding the pole in the other. The animal brayed loudly in protest as it began to inch forward into the river. The determination of the men seemed to force the animal into a state of submission, one Izar had not managed to achieve. Izar cautiously followed the route taken by the donkey. The dog too appeared to be more convinced about crossing the water and, with its head held high, started to paddle, following the others.

All three humans stumbled on the uneven surface, but it was most difficult for Izar. When the rock under his good leg rolled, he was unable to resume his balance with the weakened one. He shouted as he once more fell and splashed into the cold water. Desperately, he fought the current of the river to regain his balance, mindful of how the turbulence had seized Lin. With relief he felt the firm hand of the man, who had been following the donkey, as he grabbed Izar's arm and pulled him to his feet.

"You are too young to die. Hold on to the pole."

Izar spluttered words of thanks as he gripped the pole.

"Saving your life is good payment for use of your donkey," shouted the man. Both of them laughed.

The dog was first across and stood shaking the water off its coat as the others climbed up the riverbank. There, they lifted the deer off the wet donkey and tied it once more onto the pole.

"Where are you going, boy?" asked one of the men.

"I don't know, but I must travel in a direction with the sunrise behind me, as far as possible."

"Why?"

"Because, like the deer, I am being hunted."

"I hope you have better fortune than the deer," he said.

Both men laughed again.

"You are wet and there is not enough warmth in the sun now for you to get dry before a cold night comes. Join us and come to our village. You can dry your clothes and share some of the deer."

The other man added, "But we must hurry to be there before the darkness comes and our kill attracts four-legged hunters."

Izar was already feeling the discomfort of the wet clothing and, after some hesitation, accepted the men's invitation.

"I fear that I walk too slowly to keep up with you. I must ride on the donkey."

"So be it, here let me help you get on."

The red rays of the sunset could still be seen over the top of the mountain as they emerged from the forest of black pine trees and joined a trail, which very soon led into a small village. Their coming was heralded by the barking of dogs and the screaming of excited children who rushed out to meet the hunters. They marched on either side of the deer as it was paraded for the villagers to see. In the centre of a group of thatched huts a large fire was already lit in anticipation that the hunters would have brought something home. Izar quickly climbed off the donkey and passed its rein to two young boys, who led the animal over to where others were tethered. He grabbed the dog and held it firmly as it introduced itself to the village dogs with much sniffing and tail wagging.

The hunters' women had come out of their huts to greet their men.

"We found this boy, though looking at his hands he is more of a young man, wandering the forest, he is wet. Dry his clothes. He will eat with us."

One of the women replied, "We have no space for him in our hut."

The other replied, "There are no children in ours, he can sleep on our floor."

These were very welcome words to Izar, who was extremely tired.

While they were speaking, other women had already hung up the deer by its hind legs and, having slit open its stomach, were gutting it, ready to hack off pieces to roast on the fire. The village dogs excitedly clamored round a pile of entrails that had been thrown to them.

Izar pulled off his wet leather jacket and passed it to one of the hunter's women, to hang in front of the fire. He suddenly realised that he still had the knives in his quiver, which he had taken off his belt and placed on the ground with the bag and his bow. In his tired state, absentmindedly, he pulled one of the knives out of the quiver to dry it by the fire. The action was noticed by a boy of about the same age as him. He came closer to look at what Izar had in his hand.

"Is this a knife?" he asked.

Izar immediately became alert.

"Eh, yes, but not like we are used to," he said as he fumbled, trying to put the knife back into the quiver.

"Let me see," insisted the young man loudly.

His raised voice attracted the attention of one of the hunters.

"Why do you shout at the boy? What do you want to see?"

"He has something mysterious; he has put it in his quiver."

Looking at Izar, he said, "What does he mean? What are you hiding?"

The man bent over to take the quiver from Izar, but he snatched it away. It was no good, the man's inquisitiveness would have to be satisfied, and not just his, as very quickly a crowd had gathered to see what was hidden in the container.

Reaching into the quiver, Izar felt the bone handle of the knife and slowly pulled it out.

CHAPTER 9

People in the crowd craned their necks to look over each other as Izar held the knife up. At first, they were pushing towards him to get sight of the object, but then, as Izar held it higher, they recoiled as one and sought to keep distance between themselves and the shiny implement.

"What manner of stone is this knife made of?" asked the hunter.

Izar had thought that people would be interested in or perhaps surprised at the sight of the knife, but he had not expected such a strong reaction from the crowd. He instantly recognised that the implement in his hand was an object that caused much more wonderment than he had expected and not just that, but also great consternation among the people. What he had not yet realised, but soon would, is that the knowledge he possessed about the way the knife was made and the material that formed it, gave him great power over those who did not know or conceive that stone could be turned into another substance, which he knew as copper.

"It was once stone, but by a secret process it is changed into something else, something that can be formed into the shape of a knife."

The hunter took a step backwards. "And you know this secret?"

"Yes, and it is known only by a very small number of others."

There was a babble of conversation amongst the crowd, which was being swelled by more villagers who had heard the noise. Izar could hear comments being made about magic and him being a wizard.

"Can you teach us this secret?" asked the hunter.

Izar searched for an answer. Eventually, he replied, "The spirit of the mountain will only permit a very few to know the secret. I cannot tell you."

The crowd parted and a stooping old man with long, grey hair drooping around a fox fur over his shoulders, shuffled to the front. It was clear from the reverence the villagers showed him that he was the head man of the settlement. Despite the warmth of the evening, he wore a heavy, grey, woollen cloak. His face above his beard was creased with many wrinkles and as he opened his mouth to speak, Izar saw that he had just two teeth.

His voice quaked as he struggled to talk. "On my travels to the lands far away in the direction of the rising sun, I have seen such a thing. There some men had this magical stone in rings around their necks. They were the high priests of the spirit of the sun. Other men worshipped them, for they had the power to make the very stone of the mountain obey them to form whatever shape they wanted."

There was a gasp from the crowd.

"This boy has the same power!" he shrieked.

Those in the front row of the crowd struggled to move back further, distancing themselves from Izar. He did not know what to say, but just watched as the old man held out his hands to him in supplication. Izar could see that he had four rows of dots on his hands and three more.

"Fear not, old man, I need just food for me and my dog and a place to lay my head. Tomorrow I will leave to travel away from the rising sun."

Izar lowered the knife and put it into his quiver.

"Why are you going that way?" asked the old man.

Izar hesitated. He did not want to tell him that he was trying to escape from Rab, as he might have friends or allies here who would want to help him.

"I have been instructed to journey to where the sun sets."

"And it is the Sun God who has wished this?"

Izar thought briefly, realising that it could be to his advantage that these people believed this was so.

"It is," he lied.

"Beware, for I have heard it told that where the land ends, there is a sea and beyond that is a land of dark-haired people with such magical power that they can move mountains."

"It is the direction I must go," answered Izar.

The old man's brow was more creased than ever as he considered his reply. He slowly scratched his beard, then turned to face the crowd.

"We cannot leave this boy to travel to the end of the world alone. We should choose the strongest of our young men to go with him. The Sun God wills it."

There were shouts of approval from the crowd.

"But first, we must harvest the fields," shouted one man.

"We need the young men to help with this. We must have food for the cold time," shouted another.

There were many who expressed their views, but all agreed that Izar should have some protection in his quest to the lands where the sun set.

The old man turned to Izar and in his thin croaky voice intoned, "We shall help and win favour from the sun god. But first we will cut the stalks of our corn."

With the possibility of an escort on his journey, Izar was content to delay leaving.

The delay was, however, longer than a few days, for the villagers were not satisfied that the yellow crop in their field was yet ready for harvesting. He had been lodged in a hut with the old man who considered that it was his privilege to share accommodation with the potent stranger. The young man was well cared for and should have been happy, but the image of poor Lin kept reoccurring to him and the anguish it produced was difficult to dispel. The grief and guilt he felt did not seem to diminish.

Izar spent as many days as he had spots on his hands, waiting for the harvest to be accomplished. Just as he had done in Rab's village, he spent his time carving images, making arrowheads, walking with his dog and practising with his bow. The perfection of the images he created strengthened the view of the old man that he had special powers bestowed on him.

"I will soon die; can you craft an image of me that can be kept by my people to remind them of a great village headman?"

Izar was somewhat nervous about accepting the request, but he could see that his reputation would be damaged if he refused.

"I will try, but I must choose the wood carefully."

"What manner of wood do you need?"

"A log the length of my forearm, from a freshly felled birch tree."

"You shall have it after sunrise tomorrow."

Izar, realising how important this task was, prepared some new flint cutting blades. The next day some villagers felled the tree and hacked a log as described. First, he set about trimming it to the right shape. Having made a flat surface, he said to the headman, "You must sit on the ground near me so that I can copy your features."

As the wood carver very carefully etched the features of the old man onto the flat surface, a crowd stood around watching. Izar was intensely nervous and took meticulous care with every cut, trying to copy the many wrinkles in the face and the thin beard. The tension was eased by the positive comments of villagers as the process proceeded.

At last, when he felt he could do no more to enhance the image, Izar said, "Come, Master, look at your likeness."

Izar was aware that the only time the man might ever have seen his likeness was when he peered into a bowl of water, so it was unlikely that he could declare the carving inaccurate. He also knew that there was a risk that the green birch wood might crack when it dried, but to have used a hard wood the image would have taken very much longer to complete.

"It is indeed a fine image, Izar. You have been gifted with rare talents by the Sun God."

He held the carving up for the assembled villagers to see and declare their admiration.

Izar's status had risen even higher.

CHAPTER 10

"Now the harvest is finished, and we have enough grain for our needs and some over to trade, it is time for you to leave to do the Sun God's bidding," said the old man to Izar.

Izar was instantly alert. "You trade some of your harvest?"

"Yes, the traders come here after the hot season every year. We trade to get beakers and bowls from them."

"I must leave immediately," exclaimed Izar.

"You can wait until we have done our trade, can you not?"

"No, I need to go today."

"But the sun is already high, and the merchant's carts have been sighted near the river."

"No, it must be today that I leave. Please have the children bring me my donkey and I will gather up my possessions," said a worried Izar.

"If you insist. Then I will tell the men who will accompany you."

Shortly afterwards, the small group was ready to leave. The village men had bags with food and each was armed with a bow and arrows. Izar clambered onto the donkey's back and, after jabbing his heels into the animal's side several times and coaxed by the barking dog, it reluctantly and slowly began to follow the walking warriors. They numbered just more than the dots on one hand.

"Farewell, Izar," croaked the old man. "Travel well."

As the party made their way down through the trees, following the river, they caught sight of a large group of men with two carts, standing on the opposite bank, preparing to cross. Some of Izar's warriors waved as they turned their backs towards the newcomers and made their way towards the land where the sun set.

This was the beginning of a very long and tiresome journey. They traversed forest tracks and muddy bogs following a river valley in their quest to reach their destination. From time to time they saw small boats on the river and realised that their journey would be quicker if they had one themselves. When the food they had taken with them ran out, the men hunted for wild game and foraged for fruit and berries. When they were hunting, Izar's pace slowed them down, but they were keen to have him with them as they had seen how skilful he was with a bow. They taught him the tricks of tracking animals and also the way to dispatch big prey without risking getting too near. The hunter's secret was a purple flower, which abounded on the mountainside: monkshood. The whole plant was poisonous, but the seeds and root were so in particular. They crushed the root and very carefully smeared the juice on their arrows, avoiding getting it on their hands. The effect on a felled animal was to bring death very quickly.

They seldom met other people, but when they did, they kept their distance, mindful of their purpose in protecting their special companion. However, the journey took the villagers further and further from their home and their initial enthusiasm began to wane. As the days passed and got shorter, the men began to get anxious about the coming cold times. As they sat around their fire in the evening, one man said what they all knew.

"The sun still sets far in the distance and we have further to go. We have seen the geese flying towards the midday sun and the leaves falling from the trees. Soon the sun will lose its warmth and the world will be cold. We cannot travel then."

"We must stop at one of the settlements we have seen and ask to spend the season of snow with them," said another.

"Do you think that they would accept strangers to stay through the cold time? We have nothing to offer," said Izar.

"Any head man would be honoured to have you stay in their village."

"I am not sure of this," replied Izar. As he spoke, the dog began to growl and Izar patted it reassuringly.

"But first we must find a settlement. There is a great distance between them."

There was a long silence while they all considered how long ago it was since they last saw a village. The silence was punctuated by the growling and fretting of the dog. They paid it no attention as they concentrated on the subject of their discussion.

The one who had spoken first, a tall muscular man whom all called Yor, broke the silence, "We cannot turn back, so we'll continue until we find a place where we might spend the season of snow."

One of the other men stood up and peered down on the others in the flickering firelight. He spoke forcefully.

"I say we should turn back. Three full moons have passed while we have been travelling, yet we get no nearer to a land where the sun sets."

Three more men stood up and one of them said, "We too will turn back."

"You fools," said Yor. "You will never reach our village before the snows come."

"Yes we can if we move swiftly, not at the pace of this lazy donkey."

There was a quick succession of thuds as arrows hit the four standing men who were illuminated by the fire. Their screams were lost in the crescendo of war whoops from the attackers, hidden by the darkness, and the barking of the dog.

Before Izar could reach for his bow, men appeared out of the darkness and seized him, Yor and one other man who was still sitting and yanked them to their feet. The captured man next to Yor managed to break free and grabbed his axe, but before he could use it one of the assailants felled him with a spear. At the same time, the dog's barking stopped, for somewhere beyond the fire it had been silenced.

By the light of the flames Izar could now see some of the killers as they searched through the men's bags and wrenched out the contents.

"Why have you attacked us? We are harmless travellers," shouted Yor, showing no sign of fear.

"We have watched you for days. We protect our master from those who would harm him. Where are you going?"

"We seek the land where the sun sets."

There was laughter among the attackers.

"Can there be such a place?"

"We believe so, the boy has power from the Sun God."

"What power?"

"He can melt stone to make knives."

The men conferred between themselves. The leader said, "Come, we will show you to our master before we kill you."

The group started to move off, one of them leading the donkey.

The speaker pushed Yor and Izar to follow the attackers as they made their way along the dark track. Izar was too slow and the leader pushed him again.

"My friend cannot walk well, he must ride the donkey," said Yor in a very determined voice.

"Wait with the animal," he commanded his men.

In the gloom, Izar could just make out the shape of the donkey. He pulled himself onto its back. The leader slapped its rump and it slowly followed the men in front.

Dawn was breaking as they came over the crest of a hill and, on the riverside ahead of them, they saw a remarkable sight. Smoke was rising from huts inside a high, circular fence. This fence was made from many poles, each sharpened at the top. Neither Izar nor Yor had ever seen such a huge construction.

The party followed a trail that led up to the fence. When they arrived there, the leader called out. A gate was opened, and the group went through the entrance to the accompaniment of cocks crowing, children shouting and dogs barking.

Izar was grabbed by the leader, pulled off the donkey and thrown to the ground. Yor was likewise humiliated.

"Kneel, before our master," ordered the leader.

Izar, who could not bend his leg, sat in the mud of the walkway, while Yor knelt. The children surrounded them, shouting taunts. In front of them were many huts of different sizes. After a short time, the doorway in one of the largest was uncovered and a man pushed his way out. He was unusually tall and very broad. He wore a woven cloak, the multitude of its colours indicating that this was a man of standing. Over his chest was draped a plaited beard.

"Who have you here?" he roared at the leader of the attackers.

"Master, we found a band of men who planned to attack our village. We spared these two as there is a strangeness about them."

"Strangeness?"

"The man claims that the boy has power from the Sun God."

"Stand up, boy. Show me the power you possess."

Izar struggled to his feet and fumbled with the quiver, which still hung from his belt.

CHAPTER 11

Those guarding the prisoners held their weapons at the ready, not sure what Izar was going to bring out of the quiver. When he saw the knife, he was disappointed, for it did not look at all like it had all that time ago at the start of the journey. The gleaming copper was now streaked with green stains, caused by the wetness inside the quiver.

"This, Master," he said, lamely holding out the implement.

"What is it, boy?"

"As you see it is the form of a knife, though not made from stone."

The master grabbed it from Izar. He peered at the stained metal and turned it over in his hand.

"If you allow me to clean it, Master, I will show you more clearly the nature of the thing."

"I can feel that it is strangely smooth, not like a stone knife. But how was it made?"

Izar summoned up courage to state, "Only very few know of the secret pertaining to the melting of stone."

"Melting stone? Why, this cannot be possible."

"It is to those who have been given the gift by the Spirit of the Mountain."

"And you have this gift?"

"I have, Master, and now the Sun God wishes me to travel to the land where the sun sets, to take the knowledge there."

Izar had been using this lie for so long now that he almost believed it himself and was very convincing.

"And who is he?" said the master, pointing to Yor, who was still kneeling.

"He is my companion on the journey. Your men have killed the others of our party and my dog."

"Hold out your hands," ordered the big man.

He looked at the spots and said, "You are very young to have such knowledge. It is too late in the year for you to travel now, the cold time is coming. You and your companion will stay here until the days are longer again, and you must teach me the secret."

Izar realised that he and Yor had no option but to accept the invitation of the master, but he knew that if he betrayed the secret Rab had taught him, he would have nothing to bargain with. He was aware that they were only alive because of the master's interest in his "gift." They would have to maintain the man's fascination if they were to survive.

This fascination did indeed save their lives, but more than that, it eventually led to the master's greed being fed by the ingenuity of the two captives, as he developed some dependence on the two of them to grow his wealth and status. Their stay in the village was to be much longer than the four or five full moon periods of the cold time, much, much longer.

In the beginning, having been told that the two men needed to break open rocks and look inside them, the master sent workers to dig through the snow and search for different kinds of stones. They brought them back and cracked them open, using fire and cold water.

With Yor's help, Izar closely examined the stones brought to him. He was relieved to see that none showed signs of the greenness Rab had taught him to look for. For if he had found such rocks, he might have no option but to show the master the secrets of the process.

Their employer's patience eventually began to wear thin and there was a growing danger that he might begin to doubt Izar's ability. While they were being treated well in the village, they were in effect prisoners, servants who could be disposed of like their dead companions. And they had reason to fear the master, for they had seen how badly he treated the village folk.

Izar sensed that the situation was becoming critical and was quite terrified when the master demanded that he and Yor should go to see him.

When the pair arrived, he was standing with a group of his henchmen and was clearly in an aggressive mood.

"Why can you not show me the melting of the stone?" he demanded.

Izar's throat felt dry as he tried to hide the fear he felt and the trembling it was causing.

"The spirit of the mountain has not placed such stone in your land," answered Izar as determinedly as he could.

"Then we must find it in another place. Soon, when the ice has gone from the river, there will be merchants wishing to trade with us. Surely, they will know where such stone is to be found and bring it to us."

Izar hesitated for a moment. He recognised from his experience with Rab that large quantities of rock had to be available to hunt through to find the green traces. It would be very difficult to transport such quantities over long distances. He had an alternative idea, but he knew it would meet with disapproval and perhaps fury. He summoned up courage and then said, "It would be best if you could trade with the merchants for copper. There are mines in the high mountains and surely there must be a supply of copper."

"But then I would not see the melting of stone you talk about," he roared.

There were comments and some grumbling from the other men as they agreed with their leader.

Izar felt very intimidated, for he knew that his life depended on the big man's goodwill. He had to think quickly about how he could keep it. He swallowed, took a deep breath and then said, "No, we would not melt the stone, but my suggestion would lead you to become even more wealthy and for your village to achieve fame."

"How would this be?"

"With the copper I could, with Yor's help, make blades such as the one I have shown you. These would be very valuable and you could take advantage of the lust of other village leaders to own these mystical things."

The master scratched his beard as he considered the young man's long speech. He turned and consulted some of the men. He turned back and said loudly, "Are you sure you can make these things?"

"Yes, I am."

The group was impressed by the young man's confidence and several urged the headman to agree to the proposal.

"Then we will do so. Begin immediately."

"I will, as soon as we can get some copper."

Word was sent out to the neighbouring villages that they wanted to trade for the metal. The message quickly spread throughout the region and several months later merchants appeared seeking to trade raw copper.

Under Izar's direction and the constant assistance of Yor, charcoal burners were built and hearths constructed. It had not been easy to put into practise the skills Rab had taught him. It took many weeks to perfect the process of making objects from the molten metal. The two men experimented with different techniques to prevent the casts becoming brittle. They also had problems getting a smooth surface on the cast: at the beginning it was porous, with many tiny holes. By changing air flow through the hearth and making other small adjustments they eventually mastered the art of producing knife blades that could be polished to a shining finish.

Rumours about the work of the metal smith began to circulate in the region and interest in acquiring one of the mystical copper knives grew. Soon, visitors started to come to the village, eager to trade. As the metal smith had recognised, the knives themselves were not as sharp or even as strong as tools made of flint, but the value in them was the mystery of their production. Only men of substance could afford to have them, and their attraction was the extra status they bestowed on the owner.

The production of the implements, though never great in number, became important in increasing the prowess of the master. As Izar had predicted, the trading of the blades also brought him material reward. Despite the cost, demand was constant and even increasing as clan leaders demanded that their copper knives should be included in their grave goods when they or other influential people died.

Many villagers were employed in the supply of the timber required by Izar for his magical work. The sound of axes echoed through the forest as sapling black pine trees, which abounded in the valley, were felled and cut. Teams of men dragged the wood to the charcoal clamps outside of the village wall where the burners, figures almost permanently covered in soot, tended the fires. While he had to divulge how the wood should be slow burned with little air supply to produce the vital black fuel, he shared knowledge of producing the moulds and the metal casting only with Yor. It was essential that they retained this secret, for their lives depended on it.

The village was well defended from intrusion by those seeking to grab a share of the master's wealth, but it was not a happy place. Apart from his henchmen and the group of warriors who had seized Yor and Izar, all the village men spent most of their lives toiling hard in the service of the headman, and they worked in fear. There was a post in the middle of the village where those who displeased him were tied and whipped.

Izar and Yor had spent most of their time in the workshop, a shelter adjoining the house in which Izar lived. The shelter was carefully screened by hurdles to prevent observers watching the process going on in the small ovens, clay-lined pits in the ground.

The months turned into years as Izar and Yor worked to satisfy the greed of their employer. The activity was intense and always under the pressure of having to gratify their master. Izar developed physically as he became a man and, though he was never nimble on his feet, he grew in strength and dexterity from the constant toil. But the two of them derived material benefits from the work too. They both had comfortable huts and the master's servants provided them with good food. Early on in their stay, Yor met a woman to his liking and she joined him, living in his hut. As their skills improved so did their fame and status, but always hanging over them was the threat that if they lost the favour of the master, their lives could be cut short.

By the time Izar had two rows of dots on both hands, he too had found a woman to live with him. She was a villager called Rin. When she bore a son, they named him Tan. Rin had never really recovered from a difficult birth and was often sickly. But they were lucky, for many babies did not survive for long and many women died in childbirth.

It was just after Izar had four more dots on one hand that he convinced the master to let him attempt to produce the discs such as he had once proposed to Rab. He made some circular clay moulds and into each poured molten copper. He experimented for some time to make the discs both smooth and thin. His hunt for perfection caused a delay, which incensed the headman.

"You have shown that you can make knives, why do you waste time and my copper," he complained.

"But the copper is never wasted, for each time I am unable to make what I want, we can save the copper and melt it down again."

"What about the wood you waste in the fires? I want to see these discs of which you speak, that is if you can really make them."

"Please give me just a few more days, I am sure it can be done."

"You have until the full moon. If you fail, I will force you to teach others to make knives and then I will no longer need you."

Just before the allotted deadline, Izar was satisfied that he was able to make a disc just as he wanted it. He gave Yor the task of making a hole at the edge, through which a thong could be passed.

The final step in the process was for Izar to use a fine flint blade to etch a design on the disc. He chose to make the image that of the sun rising over the horizon, the design he had on his beaker.

When Izar presented the master with the copper disc the man was delighted, realising that he was the only man in the land who had such a tribute to the Sun God.

"The Sun God will be pleased that you bear a pendant with his image. It will bring you great fortune, of this I am sure," said Izar.

"Are you certain? We will see if the harvest is good, if not then you have cheated me."

"Now I can make many more such pendants for you to trade with."

"No! This will be the only one. Only I will have such a copper image."

"But, I can make other images on new discs," pleaded Izar.

"No, destroy your moulds. Mine shall be the only one."

And so Izar returned to making knife blades, and with increasing anxiety wondered how good the harvest was going to be. He was never to find out, for soon after full moon his life would change dramatically.

"Close the gate!" shouted the lookout, who stood on a platform that allowed him to see over the fence.

"But there are still women outside working the land and boys at the charcoal burners!" a man below him shouted.

"They must flee into the forest," said the armed man whose job was to identify those entering and leaving the village. "Close the gate, I say."

The master heard the commotion and hastened to the gate.

"What is it!" he bellowed. "Why are you shutting the gate in the middle of the day?"

"There are boats coming into the harbour, such craft as we have never seen before."

"How many?" demanded the headman.

"Almost as many as the fingers on both hands."

People were scurrying around. Mothers gathering up their children, men running to look out at the strangers through the narrow gaps between the fencing posts and others quickly arming themselves.

When the alarm sounded, Izar and Yor, busy at their workplace polishing some copper knives, put them down and went to find out what was happening. They too sought a gap in the posts to watch the arrival of the boat people.

"There are just two men in each boat, though they are large enough to carry more," observed Yor.

"They are approaching the gate, we should hide the knives we were working on," replied Izar.

"Look, they are placing their weapons on the ground to show that they come in peace!"

The lookout shouted out the same information to the master.

"Ask them what they want!" he called.

The lookout did so, but those inside could not hear the reply. The guard turned and called out, "Most do not speak the same way as us, but at least one of them can. He said they want to tell us about a land they come from and why they are here."

The master was intrigued. He ensured that there were plenty of armed men behind him and then shouted, "Let them come in."

Willing hands pulled open the creaking gate and the strangers entered. There was a gasp from the village people when they saw them. All their clothes were made of woven cloth, their leggings, their shirts and jackets. Some had a sheepskin collar round their necks. But what was most noticeable and had led to surprise among the villagers, was that the men had dark hair and beards, not at all like the fair-haired villagers. Not only this, but their eyes were brown, not blue. They were also tall, and most were well built. One of their number pushed through the group and addressed the master, for it was obvious who was the headman.

"Greetings. We are from a land many full moons' travel away. We are warriors from the tribe of the Duran. We come peacefully."

Though the man spoke strangely, the villagers could understand most of what he said.

The headman, who had always looked almost a giant of a man among his own people, now seemed much smaller when compared with the newcomers.

"We are of the Rhetian tribe. Why have you come to my village?" he asked.

"We come from a land where there are no snows in the cold time. A land of green fields good for farming, a place where there are plentiful animals to hunt, aurochs, deer and game birds. Our rivers are full of good fish."

"So, why are you here?" repeated the master.

"In our land we have great ability to make things from the flint, which is plentiful there. We can even make huge monuments beyond belief which please the Sun God. News of your mystical skills has reached us, we too want to use the produce of the molten stone, but we have no one with the knowledge to do so. My master has sent me here with these warriors because of this."

"You wish to learn from my people?"

"No, we come to ask your people to come with us, to teach the Duran people your skills. We offer a good life in a land of plenty to those with this knowledge who will come away with us. Such newcomers will have high status among our people."

There was a buzz of conversation that halted when the Master said, "Where is your land?"

"Where the sun sinks below the hills at the end of the day is the way to our land."

The master thought for a while and then said, "It is true that our village has become famous for our knowledge and our skill in using copper. See here, I have the sun pendant."

He held out the copper disc, which he had on the leather thong around his neck.

The visitors crowded round to look at the shining pendant.

He continued, "I cannot let those you seek, with the skill to make things with copper, leave my village, for they are needed here."

"The chieftain of my land has sent you a gift and he hoped that you will accede to our request to send us men who have this secret knowledge."

The man lifted an object out of the bag he was carrying and gave it to the master, saying, "This is the blue stone from my land, see how the light catches the colour."

The gift was a finely crafted and highly polished, ceremonial stone axe head. The Rhetian chieftain held up the present for all to admire.

"Will you not allow some of your men to come with us?" asked the visitor.

There was an awkward silence while the village leader considered his reply. Then he said, "I will allow two of my workers to go with you. You may take them and their families."

"So be it, we will leave tomorrow. The man I serve will be very thankful to you."

The headman was still somewhat nervous of the strangers and said, "Tonight, you may camp outside of the fence. Tomorrow morning, I will send the men and their families to you."

"You have my thanks. Who will these men be?"

The master looked around the crowd and saw the man he was looking for.

"Izar, come here. This is the man with the special knowledge, he will choose his best helpers to go with you."

The young man limped forward to him.

"Choose one of your charcoal burners and one of the men who polishes the copper, tell them they have been chosen to travel to the far-off land with these visitors."

Izar immediately realised that a trick was being played on the Duran visitors. While two such men would have knowledge of their individual work, they could not produce copper objects themselves and were of little value. They could easily be replaced by others to continue the work in the village. Izar dared not point this out.

"I will, Master," he replied.

"Before I leave may I see the work you do here with the copper?" asked the visitors' spokesman.

The leader hesitated for a moment, considering the request and then said, "Izar will show you what he makes, but he will not tell you of the way it is done, for he alone knows this. He has it as a gift from the Sun God."

CHAPTER 12

After his conversation with the master, the tall Duran visitor left his companions and followed Izar to the shelter where Yor was polishing a knife. The man watched for a short time, then looked behind him to be sure that he was not being overheard. He quietly said, "I am Radan. We have heard that you brought the knowledge of using copper to this village."

"Copper was unknown here before I came."

"It is said that you possess the secret of melting the stones."

"This is a gift given to me by an old man in another village."

"Would you like to come with us to the far country? You would be a great man there."

Izar hesitated and gazed in silence at the knife on the bench. The thought of a long journey to an unknown land in the company of strangers unnerved him. But then he reminded himself, his current situation was equally precarious. If the harvest was bad, his cruel employer might decide that he had been cheated and this could be very dangerous for him and Yor. It was always possible too that the master might soon forcibly extract the secrets they possessed and dispense with them.

Radan interrupted the metal smith's thoughts and said, "Well, do you accept my offer?"

"My companion, Yor, and I are not free men to choose our destinies. The headman would kill us rather than release us from working here."

"Will you come with us if the master can be persuaded?"

"You say that I would be a great man in your faraway land?"

"Yes, with power and status."

"I cannot go without my companion, Yor, and our women and children."

"Of course, they must come too."

"Then, you must persuade the man who commands my loyalty."

"Say nothing to anyone of this plan but be ready to leave tomorrow, take with you some of your work."

So saying, the man left the shelter and re-joined his countrymen.

Izar had a very restless night, wondering how the stranger could persuade the master to allow them to escape the threat once made that he and Yor would be killed if they tried to leave. He was anxious too about his wife, Rin. Would she be strong enough to make a long journey? In the evening he had talked to her about the prospect of leaving the village. He was anxious about how she would react, but surprised when she readily agreed that they should try to escape the thrall of the master. Like most of the villagers, she was frightened of him and she shared their loathing of the bully. By dawn, Izar had made his decision. He was no longer the shy, diffident youth whom Stin had rescued; he was a sturdy man, confident in himself and his abilities. The prospect of using his secret skills to work with copper in a far-off land and to gain fame and status was intoxicating and so powerful that he was persuaded that he must take this opportunity.

When the village gate was opened in the morning, the strangers were preparing to leave. The two families that Izar had chosen were waiting beside a stack of baskets containing their clothes and personal effects. The master was looking forward to saying goodbye to the unwelcome visitors and walked out through the gate to see them go. But as he stepped forward to bid them farewell, the now-armed men rushed at him and attacked his guards. The Rhetians were taken completely by surprise and had hardly time to ready their spears before the strangers, wielding stone clubs, were on them. Pandemonium broke loose amid the screams of the spectating, unarmed villagers and the howls of pain from the guard as they were felled by the burly strangers, who showed no mercy except to one – the master. He was seized and held captive by two of the men. Radan lifted the man's plaited beard and pulled the leather thong from his neck, looked at the pendant and put it on himself.

"Why do you treat me like this? What do you want?" bleated the captive.

"We want the most valuable gift you can give us," said Radan.

The terrified man was in no position to negotiate. He pleaded, "Anything, anything you wish."

"Izar and his companion wish to join us, do you agree?"

"Yes, yes, they may go."

"Izar, Yor, bring your families. Join the others leaving for the boats."

They had their goods ready in the shelter where Rin, Tan and Yor's woman and daughter were waiting. The two men ran to get them and their possessions before escaping through the gate.

Turning to the crowd that had gathered to watch the spectacle of the master's humiliation, Radan shouted, "If there are others of you who have worked with Izar and Yor, come and join us. You will find a better life in my land, you will be free men and women."

There was a buzz in the crowd and several stepped forward to volunteer. Radan addressed them, "Go, get your womenfolk and children. Bring what possessions you can carry, clothes and food. Join Izar and Yor."

After first recovering the fine polished axe head gift, the strangers dragged the master to the river with them as they followed the departing crowd towards the boats.

The heavy craft, each skilfully made from hollowed logs, had been partially pulled up onto the muddy shore. Willing hands pushed them back to slide into the river. The intending passengers waded into the water, placed their goods on board and clambered in, three passengers on each. As the last ones boarded, those guarding the master released him and also boarded. Powerless, he watched as the strangers took up their paddles and turned the boats to face downstream.

"I regret the violence these Duran people use, but it has lifted the threat that hung over us," said Yor.

"This is true, he still has his wealth, but we have kept our knowledge safe," replied Izar.

"Now you will have a chance to use your gift in the far-off land."

As they rounded a turn in the river, the fortified village disappeared from view.

When they began their long journey, the weather was good for much of the time. Each evening they stopped and camped on the shore and fished or hunted. Since they were travelling with the current, the men paddling the boats had an easy task. Things went very well until the river turned in the direction where the sun is at its highest. At this point, they abandoned their boats and started to walk towards the faraway land. Izar and Rin had great difficulty keeping up with the others. Apart from Izar's weak leg, they were also restricted by the frequent need to carry Tan. Izar had another burden to carry. In his bag he had copper knives and discs. Despite the weight, he insisted on keeping them in his possession. Had it not been for the faithful assistance and physical strength of Yor, Izar would have found the journey much more difficult. The two men had developed a brother-like relationship, and they relied on each other. By association with Izar, Yor was treated as an important person by the Duran warriors. However, all was not well. It was clear that Rin was really suffering from the physical hardship of the rough walking. Yor's woman and daughter managed much better.

The men from the land they were walking to knew how valuable Izar was to them and before long they stole a donkey from a settlement they passed for him and Tan to ride on. The donkey was not all they stole. They left little food for their victims. On some occasions, they played the same trick they had used against the master. They went into a village peacefully, leaving their weapons outside, sought the headman and gave him the fine polished stone axe head to show their goodwill. In the morning, after enjoying the village's hospitality, they collected their weapons and seized the headman, recovering the axe head to use on the next occasion. Thus, the Duran men proved themselves to be ruthless and occasionally cruel, but also resourceful. When the cold time of the year approached, they raided a small village and drove the inhabitants out, taking over the simple huts for the travellers. The way Radan and his men behaved troubled the Rhetians, for it was their way to share, not to steal. They knew that the owners of the huts in which they overwintered would have found space for the visitors.

Frequently, the Rhetian villagers debated between themselves the violent nature of their guides.

"Why are they so brutal, Yor?" asked one of the women.

"It seems to be their way to be aggressive," he answered.

"Do we really want to go to the far away country if the Duran act like this?"

"Do you think that all Duran people are like them?" asked another.

Izar was besotted by the prospect of using his skills and enjoying the status that this would bring him in the far away land, so he always tried to defuse such doubt.

"The warriors have always provided well for us, we want not for food or drink because of their resourcefulness," he argued. "Perhaps they are too unkind to the strangers we depend on, but we have to accept that."

Not all of the travellers survived that winter. As soon as the frost left the earth and it was soft enough to dig, two women and one boy were buried. One of the women was Rin. Izar grieved for her and for a time had great regret that he had taken her on this long and arduous journey. Now, he had to bring up a son, a boy who had but four spots on one hand.

The corpses were interred according to the ritual of their land. The bodies were placed on their left side, their knees bent in the position of a baby in a mother's womb and their lifeless eyes pointed in the direction from whence the cold winter winds blew. A few things that could be spared by the travellers were buried with the dead. They symbolised the returning to the ground of the things the spirits of earth and mountains had provided: flint knives, the beakers that had been made from clay and bone articles such as combs, for the land had nurtured the animals from which the bones came. From the land and the mountain these things had come, and now they were returned.

CHAPTER 13

As the cold time released its icy grip and the weather warmed, the travellers resumed their journey. Radan and his warriors had traversed this route before, on their way to find Izar. They seemed to recognise landmarks and pathways through dense forest and on mountain slopes and had a determined sense of purpose about which way to go. Often the travellers walked for several days without seeing a habitation. This meant sleeping in the open in the cold nights. For protection from the weather they built simple shelters from sapling branches, which had just enough new leaf to afford some cover. The cold was overcome by small groups huddling together, but there was no refuge from rain.

The periods between finding villages small enough for Radan's warriors to terrorise the inhabitants into providing food for the travellers, could be hungry ones and occasionally seriously so. At such times, Izar made up for his lack of mobility by his skill with his bow. The land through which they travelled was rich in game and oft times he successfully killed hares and ground birds. When the warriors ranged the forest hunting bigger animals, Izar was usually left behind. However, on one occasion when the travellers were walking in single file down a narrow mountainside path, they disturbed a bull auroch, lying dozing in the sunshine inside a gulley. The black beast raised itself to its full height, its shoulder as high as a full grown man's head. It raised its massive forward-facing horns and furiously bellowed its characteristic moo sound.

This was an opportunity the hungry walkers could not afford to miss. Some men held the auroch at bay with their spears as it angrily stamped on the ground and swept its sharp horns from side to side. While they were doing this, others tried to kill the trapped animal with their arrows. However, the beast's hide was so thick that it was impossible to penetrate its skin deeply enough to do real harm.

"Wait, keep it trapped while I prepare an arrow," called Izar breathlessly when he caught up with the hunters, having dismounted some distance away.

"It's impossible to stop it with arrows!" shouted Radan.

"Give me a chance!"

"I think we have to give up," said another warrior.

"No, I have a way," replied Izar.

He had tipped his quiver upside down, causing the arrows to fall out. Not just the arrows, but a small, leather package tied up with deer sinew. Izar quickly untied the string and opened the package. In doing so he ignored advice once given to him long ago by some other hunters, all of them now dead, except Yor. He smeared the juice from a piece of root onto an arrowhead. Picking up his bow, he used it to help him clamber up onto the top of the gulley where he overlooked the animal.

He drew back the bowstring as far as he dared and loosed the arrow at the side of the auroch. The arrow penetrated its coat and stayed sticking out if its side.

"I told you it was impossible to stop it with arrows!" shouted Radan.

"Wait, it may take some time!"

Radan was not a patient man and he did not want any of his warriors to be injured by the aggressive animal.

"Let it go, we will surely find other animals to hunt," he instructed.

His men backed away from the gulley to let it escape. As they did so, it slowly made its way forward, but it had become breathless and started to wobble as it walked. It stopped. Its head dropped and its forelegs gave way, leaving it balanced on its knees. Then it rolled over onto its side, panting and jerking in death throes. The hunters rushed forward and dispatched the bull with their spears.

A cheer arose from the famished onlookers, apart from one. Izar had collapsed on top of the rock from which he had fired. The advice he had once been given was that he should never touch the monkshood poison with his fingers, for the deadly juice can penetrate skin.

Willing hands carried Izar down to the path and laid him on his bed fur. He was fighting for breath. Very soon he began to vomit violently. Yor's woman tended to him.

"He feels very cold, cover him," she said as she felt his heartbeat. She shook her head and said to Yor, "His blood is moving very slowly."

Meanwhile, several of the warriors started to butcher the auroch. It was a daunting task. They had to carve parts of the huge body and hang them from trees where the animals of the night could not reach them.

Radan gave instructions for the travellers to prepare shelters. They would not be travelling any further for at least another day.

The delay was indeed longer than a day. After a fitful night's sleep, Izar started hallucinating. He screamed and fumed, gazing wide-eyed at apparitions others could not see. All the while he was panting for breath. Had the affliction affected any other member of the group of travellers, it is likely that they would have been left to the wolves, but Izar was the reason for their journey. Radan ensured that he was made as comfortable as possible and they bided their time at the encampment in the hope that he would recover.

It took four days before Izar recovered from the poisoning.

"You are too impetuous, you act before you think," said Yor as he sat cross-legged beside the recovering patient.

"I think of things others don't," protested Izar.

"My friends, the men from my village, the ones who died because they journeyed with you, they taught you the use of the poison and I know they warned you of its potency against humans."

"I had to act fast, the auroch might have escaped."

"You acted fast because you wanted to boast that you had knowledge the others did not."

There was a long pause before Izar said, "I can't match the physical prowess of most others, but I get respect because I have knowledge, in this case of the poison."

"And more usually because of the unique ability to perform the alchemy of making metal from stone and moulding the copper," replied Yor.

Izar quickly retorted, tetchily, "And some of that same knowledge has given you status too!"

"This is true and for that I am grateful."

There was another period of quiet before Izar added, "But I did the right thing, the meat from the auroch has provided food for all of you for several days."

"True, but if you had died, there would have been no reason for us to make this journey and Tan would have been an orphan. Be careful in future. Do you know what my tribe call this poison?

"No."

"Wolfbane, the killer of wolves. But it has another name: the "king of poisons." Take care in future, my star and yours are intertwined. The gods have decreed it so. We can do great things."

"I believe too that this is so. Tomorrow, we will resume our quest to prove it."

Radan was anxious to make up for the time they had lost and so hurried the travellers along relentlessly. Even though he was mounted, Izar in his weak state had to frequently stop for a rest.

"Walk with Izar, we'll move on," Radan instructed Yor each day. "We'll prepare the shelters and light a fire at our stopping place for when you catch up."

"If paths cross ours, leave marks to show which way you have turned," Yor always reminded Radan. He was fearful that when the main group was far ahead and out of sight, the pair of them might lose the direction of their travel, for other trails often crossed theirs.

Yor carried a spear as well as his axe and Izar had his bow. They were mindful that the two of them alone could easily become prey to a pack of hungry wolves or a bear just emerging from hibernation.

The pair spent many hours talking together as they trailed behind the others, and often they speculated about the place they were going and what they would find there. They also discussed the work that they had been doing together at the village, which was now far behind them.

"Without our advice, the master will find it difficult to check the quality of the copper the traders want to sell him," stated Yor.

"Yes, I fear that he may be cheated. Those selling the metal will realise that the men working with casting have no expert knowledge," answered Izar.

"Where do you think the best copper came from?"

"Far away in the direction of the rising sun."

"In the faraway land we are seeking, have they copper stones?" asked Yor.

"I hope so, Radan says they can get the stones we need."

"Can we trust him?"

"Without the green rocks there will be no copper," answered Izar. He added, "Why would his master send him to our lands to look for the knowledge we have, if he has no green stone?"

"But he would not know about the green stone."

This comment gave Izar cause for thought and some anxiety.

In between their conversations, Izar lapsed into reflecting deeply about what he had admitted to Yor. It was true, there was a thrill in having knowledge others did not. While his enquiring mind and ambition drove him to develop his skills, and thus status, he was also partly motivated by the fact that the prowess the knowledge and experience gave him compensated for the fact that he was not able to run or even walk fast. He wondered how he would use his skills in the faraway country. He discussed his ideas with Yor, but retained the sense that he alone was the honoured possessor of much of the knowledge imparted to him by Rab, and it should stay that way. While Yor had learned the casting process, he had not had the chance in the place they had left to produce copper. Izar alone knew how to identify the right rocks, stones that would yield the hot liquid that could be formed into shapes at his bidding.

"Yor, the blades we made are very special and men crave to own them, but as a tool or a weapon, they do not keep their cutting edge. Our knives are less useful than flint to cut and scrape."

"This is true, but the knives are not used for these purposes by the owners, they are displayed or even flaunted to impress others," said Yor.

"But if some green stones can be made to give up their secret contents, might there not be other rocks that contain different, new materials? Stones that could hold metal that would give a harder, finer cutting edge than copper?"

"Izar, sometimes you dream too much. If such stones existed, they would have been discovered by the wise man who taught you your skills," answered Yor.

"But it is possible that such stones have not yet been found. Consider too, if there might be something, perhaps another kind of metal, which could be mixed with the liquid copper to make it stronger and more long lasting. Then we could make sharper weapons and tools."

Yor was used to these conversations with Izar but was not given to speculating about such things. Nevertheless, for the sake of their friendship, he endured Izar's frequent flights of fantasy. There was also another thing that frequently occupied Yor's thoughts: his woman was pregnant and it would not be long before she again faced the danger of childbirth. He was greatly worried that the risk would be even worse if they did not reach their destination soon and she could have the help of a village birthing woman.

It was just before the time when the days were longest that the party that had travelled through forests, over mountains, across swamps and fields, in wind, rain, snow and heat, with horror saw that they could go no further. They had reached the end of their world, for in front of them was a lake of immense proportion filled with blue-green water, and beyond it was nothing. The formidable sea stretched all the way to where it met the horizon.

CHAPTER 14

"Radan, you have cheated us! There is no faraway land, only water!" complained Yor.

He spoke for all the group; they were as shocked as he was to see this unimaginably empty and wide stretch of white-flecked, greeny blue in front of them.

"Yes, where is the land you speak of?" demanded Izar.

His question was echoed by others as they crowded round Radan. He held his hand up to try to quell the rebellion. It took some time before he could make himself heard.

"This is the sea between my land and yours. We will cross it, but not here."

"We can't see any land in the distance," complained Yor.

There was a rumble of agreement from the others.

Radan continued. "We must travel further, with the midday sun on our backs, along this shore. We will come to a place where, on a fine day, my land can be seen."

"And how then will we cross this water?" asked Izar.

"We have a way, you will see."

"I think we should turn back to our homes!" shouted one woman.

Some agreed with her, but most realised the futility of trying to find the distant place where their journey had begun. However, the loudest protest came from Yor's woman.

"I will not cross this water. I am soon to give birth, Yor, you must find a place for us to stay. Somewhere we can live, a safe place where the baby and I can have a chance to survive."

Yor tried to pacify her, but he knew she was right. He turned to face Radan and asked, "How many days must we walk until we find this place of which you speak?"

Radan conferred with his men and then turned to face the group.

"We must walk the number of days you have fingers on one hand to reach the place where we will cross the sea. If the weather is bad, perhaps longer."

Izar tried to make light of the situation. He realised that at this point they had no choice but go along with these men and face the terrifying prospect of voyaging across the water to the land they could not yet see.

"We have travelled so far, a small number of days more will be nothing in comparison with the time we have been journeying," he said.

With varying degrees of enthusiasm, the fair-haired mountain people agreed. However, Yor was tormented with anxiety. He was to some extent relieved when Radan said, "On our way to the place where we will cross the water, we will stop at a village to meet another who has the knowledge of changing stone into this new material you call copper."

Izar's reaction was quite different. "But you have not told us of this man before!" he exclaimed with surprise.

"He will also come with us to the land of the Duran."

Izar was dumbfounded. "Why did you bring us on this long journey if you already have one with the knowledge I have?"

"You will see when you meet him," replied Radan.

Izar was possessed with anger, but he said no more as gradually his fury was overcome by the intriguing thought that there may be some value in finding out what skills this man had.

The following day, the group turned to follow the coast in a direction where their shadows went before them. The distance between villages was now much shorter than it had been in their earlier journey and each evening the travellers found shelter in a coastal village or hamlet. The people who lived in these habitations were mainly fisher folk, though the women also tended animals and fields of corn. Radan knew that he was now in an area where there were many more people and his warriors were highly outnumbered. He was cautious not to offend the villagers they met. But the Rhetians and the Duran could not expect free hospitality and so, in payment, offered their services helping in the fields or gutting fish. Radan's prediction that they would cross the water in five days proved to be optimistic, and one reason for the delay was to be their meeting with Old Man Zef.

It was late in the afternoon when the group of travellers neared a large village. On its outskirts, there were two large smoking stacks of wood.

"Izar, these are charcoal clamps, they must be," said Yor.

"Yes, surely they must. But why do they need charcoal here?"

"There can be but one reason."

They were overheard by Radan, who said, "Yes, this is the village of the man I spoke of."

"Why did you not tell us before?" asked Izar.

"Because when I mentioned this man's skills, you were angry."

There was a sullen silence that hid the two Rhetians' excitement about the imminent meeting.

Always when they approached a settlement, they were at first viewed with some alarm by the inhabitants, and with good reason, for the villagers feared robbers who might attack and steal.

But suspicion turned into welcome, when Radan was recognised; clearly, he was well known to the villagers.

As the fair-haired mountain people and the Duran warriors awkwardly stood in a clearing surrounded by the round huts of the villagers, they waited to see where they were to be offered hospitality. Radan spoke to the village headman in the Duran language, but Izar found that they spoke too quickly for him to understand much, even though he had learned many words during the long journey.

He turned to Izar and said, "We'll stay here for two nights. After the second night we'll leave. Tomorrow, in payment, we will help with the launching of the fishing boats and the building of some huts.

Izar was acutely aware that his lack of mobility would make these jobs difficult for him. He asked, "But what can I do to help?"

"You are not going to help, tonight you will meet Old Man Zef. I have told the headman of your skills and he wants you to meet Zef."

"Where is he?"

"You will meet him soon; I will interpret for you."

Izar was still slightly annoyed by the concept of there being a person who might rival his own knowledge, but his curiosity about the man and his work got the better of him.

"We will all sleep where there is some space in different houses, as we usually do, but you and Tan will stay with me next to the home of Zef," said Radan.

"What about Yor?" asked Izar.

"He can meet Zef tomorrow, the old man is frail and meeting two of us will be enough. Leave Tan with Yor's woman. Come, follow me."

Izar followed Radan through the village to a round hut, which was larger than the others. Attached to it was a shelter, not unlike the one where Izar used to work.

The doorway was blocked by a hurdle of interwoven stems of hazelwood. Radan leaned towards the hurdle and called out, "Hello, it is me Radan, with a stranger who possesses the knowledge you have!" They waited and soon there was the sound of the fence being moved. As it opened, they saw a woman pushing it. She beckoned to the two men to follow her. Radan went in before Izar. The room they entered was lit by several lanterns; nevertheless it took them both a while to see anything in the dim light.

The sound of a man's voice directed their attention to a low bed against the far side of the room. The weakness of the voice was in keeping with the appearance of the frail figure half sitting, propped up by rolls of animal furs behind him.

Izar waited impatiently while Zef conversed slowly with Radan, his croaking voice frequently breaking into a cough.

On one occasion he raised his voice to what, for him, must have been its maximum effect. Long ago Izar and Yor, through listening to Radan and the warriors, had begun to pick up the meaning of many words and phrases in their language. Now, because Zef spoke so slowly, Izar could understand most of what was being said, though it was sometimes necessary to have Radan translate for him.

At length, the Duran turned to Izar and said, "Sit down on the floor. Old man Zef greets us and wanted to know why we have come to see him. I reminded him that he was to come with us to my land, but he protests that he is too old and weak. I fear he is right."

Radan was interrupted by Zef; it was clear the old man wanted to ask a question.

"What does he want?" asked Izar.

"I had told him that you were also a magic man with the power to change rock to copper."

"What did he say? I couldn't understand," demanded Izar impatiently.

"He wants proof, he doesn't believe me, even though I showed him the shining disc I took from your old master."

Izar was becoming irritated; he could understand much of what the old man said but could not easily express himself. He impetuously delved into his bag and felt around inside.

"Here, show him this," he said, passing a copper knife to Radan.

The Duran passed the implement to Zef. He grabbed it and despite his weakness, suddenly sat up, galvanised by what he saw. He strained to lean towards the lamplight so he could examine the blade.

Looking at Radan, he said something in a falsetto voice with as much energy as he could muster.

"He wants to know who made this," said Radan.

Pointing to himself, Izar said, "It was me."

Zef looked at Izar intently, surprised that the younger man could use his language, albeit at a simple level. He shouted to the woman who had shown them into the hut. She immediately scurried across the reed-covered floor. Her hand delved into a basket. She passed the object she retrieved to Zef. With a shaking hand, he in turn held it out for Izar to look at.

The Rhetian was trying to hide his excitement as he took the knife and started to examine it. Zef watched him intently. After what seemed a long while, the old man said something directly to Izar. The young man looked blankly at him, not understanding entirely what had been said.

Izar looked at Radan and asked, "Did he say my knife is not good?"

"No, he said that your knife is good, but the finish is not as good as his," interpreted Radan.

At first Izar did not reply, but after some more time spent examining the blade, Izar said, rather reluctantly, "Tell him, it is true. The surface of his knife is smoother."

The old man instantaneously relaxed and collapsed back into his half-lying position. He then mumbled something to Radan.

"He said that he wants to see you tomorrow morning."

"Yes, I thought that's what he said, tell him I'd like that," answered Izar.

The two visitors stood up as Radan replied to Zef to accept the invitation to meet the next day. The woman pulled away the hurdle at the door and the men lowered their heads to get through the opening and into the last of the evening's sunlight.

"How could you have expected this old man to travel with you to your land? He is very weak and perhaps ill," said Izar.

"When I found him, long ago, at the beginning of my journey, he was much stronger. Nevertheless, I realised that he would not live many more cold seasons and my master would not be pleased with me if I only returned to him with one so old. That is why I journeyed further, much further to also find a younger man with the knowledge we needed."

"But why would the people of the village permit Zef to leave? His knowledge brings status and honour to this place."

"This is true. My master offered great wealth to this headman to let Zef go with me. The village headman agreed because Zef had a son to whom he had given his knowledge, and he would have stayed here and continued Zef's work. But now the headman has changed his mind."

"Why?"

"His son has been killed."

"Killed! How?"

"I don't know, I will ask Zef tomorrow. But if he will not come with us, you must learn all you can of his wisdom."

"Can we take Yor with us tomorrow so that he too can learn?"

"Yes, this would be a good thing. You must both learn all you can from Zef as quickly as possible. I fear that my master will be angry that is has taken so long for me to return with someone with the knowledge he seeks. Tell me, when we reach my village, Durotrin, how long will it take you to make the copper knives?"

Izar was taken aback by the question. "This depends on many things."

"What things?"

"I must have a workplace and we need much wood to burn."

"You will get these things, and when you have them how long will it take?"

"If you have a good supply of the copper rocks, it will take several full moons. If you don't, then it may take a long time to find such stones."

Radan was quiet for some time and then said, "I have no knowledge of such rocks. Is there not a quicker way?"

"Yes, we could do as Yor and I did with our previous master."

"What was that?"

"He could find no copper rocks in his land, so he traded corn and furs for raw copper, which traders brought. We made the copper pure and used it to make things."

"If necessary, this is what we will do too," said Radan firmly.

CHAPTER 15

It was not long after sunrise, that Izar, Yor and Radan went to the big hut. Once more the woman opened the hurdle gate to permit them to go in. Zef was sitting on a thick log that had been fashioned to support his back. The three men sat down on the reeds covering the floor, at the feet of the old man. After greetings had been exchanged, Zef looked suspiciously at Yor and said something gruffly to Radan. The Duran replied at length.

"He wanted to know who Yor is, didn't he?" Izar asked Radan.

"Yes, he is afraid that too many will learn the secrets of your work. But I explained that Yor was your skilled assistant. He seems happy with that."

"Ask him about his son," said Izar.

Radan asked the old man the question. The man's previously cheery face changed. His lips began to tremble and his eyes glazed over as he seemed to be experiencing a painful memory.

With a very quiet voice and slow deliberate speech, he said something solemn to Radan. The speech went on for quite a time and Izar missed much of it. Radan turned to Izar and said, "Zef's son was killed in an accident with the liquid copper. The old man is ashamed to tell you this because the accident does not reflect well on the way he taught his son the secrets he shares with you."

"What happened?"

"The son had made a new hearth, a deep hollow in the ground. Although he had lined the hollow with clay, it was not thick enough," related Radan.

"Oh no, and he had not cleared all the stones from the ground first?"

"Exactly."

"This is very dangerous. The stones can crack if the extreme heat reaches them," gasped Izar.

"What happens?"

"The shards of hot, sharp stone can fly out of the fire and hit anyone nearby. They may be seriously cut."

"I see, that is what he meant then when he told me that the Earth God did not like his son and took revenge for him disturbing the ground," said Radan.

There was a long silence, which was broken by Zef. He spoke very slowly and deliberately with a loud voice that belied his physical condition. The two Rhetians were able to understand a lot of what he said.

"As I told you the day before this one, your knife was not a good as mine. It has a line around it from the cast. Tell me, how do you make such moulds?"

Speaking directly to Zef with his halting Duran language and sometimes with the help of Radan, Izar explained how they pressed a knife into wet clay, first one side and then the other to make a mould, which they then baked.

"But why do you do this? When you put the two halves together to pour in the copper, you will always have a mark where the two parts join."

Izar was irritated to have his method, his own invention, questioned.

"This works well for us. We use sand to rub away the line that marks the blade."

Zef annoyed Izar further when he said, "This work is unnecessary if you use a better way."

Yor, who knew Izar so well, could sense his friend's anger and sought to pacify him by saying, in Zef's language, "It will be useful for us to learn from this wise old man."

Zef liked what Yor had said and smiled at him. He looked directly at Izar and said, "Your assistant is also wise. Learn from me, for I can help you. The more knowledge you have, the better it will be for you in the life you will have in the land of the Durans."

Izar took a deep breath and attempted to be humbler as he said, "Yes, you are right, for I have for many days been considering how to improve our process."

"I think we do not need Radan to help us understand each other, for I do not want to share my knowledge with anyone other than those who already have the gifts we have. Leave us Radan, I will talk with these two."

The Duran stood up and, diplomatically, made for the door without saying anything. The hurdle was lifted for him and the other three men were left alone together.

"Help me to stand up, we will go to the place where I work," said Zef, pointing at a door behind him.

The two younger men stood up, Yor more easily than Izar, and each took one side of him. Together, they shuffled to the door leading them to the workplace.

With some excitement the two Rhetians looked at the scene before them. There were several hollows in the ground where copper had been melted, and a blow bag was by one of them. On a work bench some pieces of raw copper were awaiting melting. There was also a very large clump of brown substance and a number of flint knives. Under the bench were hollowed logs containing lumps of clay. At the end of the bench, on the ground, was a pile of charcoal.

"This looks very much like the workplace we had in the village we left," said Yor.

"Yes, but look at the blow bag," said Izar, pointing to a leather pouch on the ground.

"It has two sticks to hold on to. This would be easier to use than ours," replied Yor.

Izar looked at Zef and said very slowly and deliberately, "What do you use to make the blow bag?"

"The hide of a goat is best; it is softer than that of a cow."

As the Rhetians looked around, Zef was watching them closely, especially Yor.

"What's this?" asked Izar as he walked across to the bench. He closely examined the brown clump.

"Ah, you noticed. That is why my blades are better than yours," retorted Zef.

"But how? What is it?" said Izar as he touched the brown mass.

"Beeswax, ordinary beeswax. The use of the wax is a secret I brought with me when I came to this village. For, you see, I am not a native of this land. I come from a place many days' walk away, where the sun is much hotter."

"Why did you come here?" asked Yor.

"I fled my village when it was attacked by wild men from beyond the mountains where I lived. In that place, there is plentiful stone for making copper. If you ever need any, you can trade with my people, for now they live in peace."

There was a short silence before Izar said, "Will you tell us how the beeswax is used?"

"No, not yet. I want to talk with Yor. Izar, you will leave us. Come back when the sun is higher."

Izar was at first shocked, and then anger welled up in him. Yor saw this and took Izar aside.

"Izar, please, we must do as Zef asks. I'll meet you later. His request is very mysterious."

Izar glared at his friend, exhaled loudly and then walked back through the hut and onto the path outside. He felt insulted, he was the man who had been gifted the knowledge, it was he who should be talking with Zef. His mood did not change until he met Tan, who was playing outside their lodging hut.

Later, as instructed, Izar returned to Zef's hut. He was once more admitted by the woman. She ushered him through the hut and out into the workshop. He immediately recognised the smell of charcoal fumes. There, in front of him, Yor was on the ground.

Looking at the crouching figure, Izar asked, "What are you doing, Yor?"

"He is showing me what he knows about melting copper," said Zef, who was sitting on a bench, watching Yor.

"This wind bag is very good, I have quickly reached the point when the copper will do as I command it," commented Yor.

"You can stop now. We must talk," instructed Zef.

Yor stopped pumping the bag and let the fire begin to die down as he stood up and brushed ash from his leggings.

Izar bent over the fire to inspect the copper in the clay crucible. Then he stood up and said, "So, why did you ask Yor to do this?"

Zef stroked his beard and said, "Izar, I see from your work that you are a very clever man, but I can make you even more clever."

Izar was now conscious that he should be respectful to this old man, more respectful than he had been earlier in the day, if he were to benefit from this chance meeting with one so experienced.

"It is true that I would like to learn from your wisdom and knowledge."

"Izar, you have a problem as indeed do I. But by solving your problem you can remove mine. However, everything has a cost and I will repay you for making my heart lighter by teaching you what you need to know."

The Rhetian was irritated by this oblique statement but tried to retain his composure.

"Zef, you speak in riddles, words with a meaning I cannot understand."

"Ever since my son could walk, he has worked with me and learned from my wisdom. And I was happy, happy because I knew that everything I had taught him would be passed on to his children and to theirs. The knowledge would give them status, importance and good things in life."

Zef paused and momentarily focused on a personal vision his visitors could not possibly see.

"My son is dead. All I have taught him is wasted. There is no one to take my place in this village, for it must be so that soon I will be laid to rest."

The two Rhetians were silent, for neither had grasped where the old man's logic was taking him.

"I want Yor to be my assistant. He can be my stepson; he will inherit my place in this village."

"But he is my assistant," stuttered Izar.

"Yes, but how will you solve your problem?" asked Zef.

"What problem?"

"Izar, I see what Zef is saying. You have your mind so deeply involved in your work that you have not noticed," said Yor.

"What, noticed what?"

"In two days Radan will be taking us all across the wide water to his land. My woman refuses to make this journey. She will give birth very soon. We cannot travel, for if the baby is born on the journey it will surely die as may she."

Once more there was silence. It was broken by Zef.

"So, by keeping Yor here with me, I solve your problem and by him being here, my legacy is assured."

"But Yor is very important to my work, he helps me greatly," complained Izar.

"And that is why I say that the cost will be repaid. I will recompense you with knowledge, knowledge that one day you can pass to your son. But we must ask Yor how he feels about this solution to our difficulties."

They looked at Yor as he reached for words.

"I am honoured to work with Izar. He has taught me, a simple village boy, so much. But Zef, the opportunity you offer me is one I would like to accept. But I cannot do so without the goodwill of Izar."

Zef was not finished with his persuading of Izar; he interrupted and said, "Izar, you must consider too that in a way this has worked out well for you. For if I had been well enough to travel to the land of the Durans, I would have been the "special one," and even if only Yor had accompanied you, then you would have to share the status of being the owner of the mysterious knowledge."

"This is difficult for me, not only has Yor helped me so much with my work, but I also rely on him at times to help me when my leg causes me trouble."

"But, Izar, you are so much stronger now, you walk well and though you cannot run you can manage to travel without help," said Yor. "And Tan is growing fast, he will be able to help you more each day."

"How old is your son?" asked Zef.

"He will have all the fingers on one hand marked this warm time."

"Then he is old enough to begin to learn this work."

There was a short silence, terminated by the sound of Izar taking a deep breath and then saying, "So be it then, but Yor, can you help me to get into the boat when we shall cross the sea?"

The other two men's faces creased into a smile and Yor nodded.

"You have but today before Radan requires you to leave. You must ask him to change his mind so that you can stay one more day. We have much to do to perfect the way you make your copper moulds, for this is what I can teach you," said Zef.

"Yes, but I have already realised that the secret involves the use of beeswax," replied Izar.

Zef laughed and said, "You are right. We will start with the blade you have shown me. Put it on the bench."

The old man slowly stood up and shuffled to the bench. He picked up a flint blade and said, "Yor, cut a piece of beeswax just longer than the copper knife."

Yor did as requested.

"Izar, now use the flint to make a beeswax copy of your blade."

This was a task that Izar immediately warmed to and, using his carving skills, within a short time had made a good copy of the knife. Meanwhile, Zef had directed Yor to take some clay and, mixing it with water, make a thick paste.

"Yor, bring the fire back to life, put on more charcoal."

Izar was intrigued by what Zef would ask for next, for surely if he put the beeswax carving by the fire, it would melt.

"Now, Izar, use the bristles on that piece of cow's hide to gently smooth the clay onto the carving, but keep one end open by inserting this twig, and at the other end place this thinner one."

Zef passed Izar the twigs and he did as he was instructed, covering the whole copy of the blade with the creamy paste.

"Put it by the fire, not too close or it will crack. When it has dried a little on both sides, smooth more clay onto the copy."

And so they proceeded for some time until the original beeswax carving was covered by a thick clay casing.

"Now, we must leave the cast to dry out overnight."

"You call this the cast?" asked Izar. "There is no void in which to pour the molten metal."

"Yes, at this time, this is so. Now I am very tired and I must sleep. Remember, tell Radan that you must stay one more day. Come back here early tomorrow."

The two men left the workshop and walked through the hut out onto the pathway. They were both aware that their relationship had changed and there was some awkwardness between them, which Yor attempted to overcome by saying, "Izar, we have been close friends and endured many difficulties and dangers together. I thank you for your wise teaching and for giving me this opportunity."

"Yor, we can still be friends, but now we are also rivals. Only time will show which will be stronger, our friendship or our rivalry."

There was a long silence as they walked to the huts where they would be sleeping; it was broken by Izar, who said, "Now I must persuade Radan to allow me to stay another day."

CHAPTER 16

"No, this is not possible, we must move on, we have been delayed too much already. The master is an impatient man. We must leave in the morning," said Radan, his voice raised with annoyance. "You have had all of this day to learn from Zef, that must be enough."

"But unless I stay for a day, Yor will have more knowledge than me. He will learn things I cannot."

"What do you mean?"

"Yor is staying with the old man, to become his assistant."

"Is he not travelling with us?"

"No, his woman is refusing to go. But he will go with us as far as the place where we must enter the sea."

Radan calmed down and said, "This is a good thing, for she complains too much about danger."

Izar was getting another insight into Radan's ruthless nature and silently, with much resentment, prepared himself to creep into the cot he shared with Tan. Sleep did not come easily as he tortured himself with thoughts of the next step in Zef's procedure, one he was never to see. He would have to find out himself.

The next day, soon after sunup, Radan gathered his men and with the Rhetians set off, following the coast line. Yor walked beside Izar and they conversed all day about their meeting with Zef. The awkwardness between them of the day before had dissipated as they enthusiastically reflected on what the future might hold for each of them.

Just before sunset the band of travellers came to a settlement from which it appeared that the sea did have an end, for in the far distance there was a thin line between the sea and the sky.

"There is our land," said Radan, pointing at the horizon.

"But how can we cross this sea?" asked Izar.

"Come, we must talk to men in this village and arrange boats to take us," he replied.

They walked through the group of huts towards the water's edge.

Radan pointed at two vessels, which were pulled up onto the stony shore. "Here are the boats that will take us across to the far country."

The intending passengers moved forward to inspect the craft.

"Can these boats cross such a sea with waves like those?" asked Izar, pointing first at the boats and then the sea.

"Yes, they are strong, look at the way they are made," answered Radan.

Izar and Yor inspected one of the boats. Unlike those they had travelled in from their village, which were large, hollowed logs, these had flat planks that had been skilfully fashioned to a similar thickness. There were four planks side by side in the bottom of the boat and two that ran around the sides, though these were made in several pieces.

"How are the planks joined? What stops them from falling to many pieces when the boat hits a wave?" asked Yor.

Two men from the settlement, who had been watching the group and listening to the conversation, stepped forward. One of them said to Yor, "Come, look at this."

The man bent over the side of the boat and pointed at the floor. "Each plank is bound together by knots of withy."

"The planks are sewn together with the strips of willow wood," stated the other.

"And how is the sea kept out of the boat?" asked Izar.

"When the planks are wet, in the sea water, they grow bigger by a small amount. Then the joints are tight."

"So, the sea cannot enter the boat?" asked Yor.

"Only a very little."

"Look, out to sea, here comes a boat!" shouted Radan.

They all turned to look. In the distance was a boat coming towards them. As it slowly got closer, they could see that there were four men paddling, two at the front and two at the back. Eventually, when it came close to the shore, the two men who had been telling Izar and Yor about the boat construction waded into the water and helped the arrival through the surf and onto the beach. The men on board jumped out and the six of them dragged the heavy boat ashore.

"There are no passengers," said Izar. "But look, the boat is carrying goods."

In the middle of the vessel were several large bales, wrapped in animal skins that were sewn together to keep the contents dry.

When the six men had unloaded the bales, one of them came to Radan.

"You all want passage to the other side?"

"Yes."

"How many are you?"

Radan held up both hands with his fists clenched. He unclenched his hands three times, showing all his fingers, and then held up one hand showing three fingers.

"What will you pay me with?" asked the boatman.

Radan turned to Izar. "You have a good knife of copper in your bag?"

"Yes, but…"

Radan interrupted him and said, "Give it to me."

Izar delved into his bag and took out a knife. He handed it to Radan.

"We pay with this," said Radan to the boatman.

The man looked astounded and peered at the knife. "I have heard of these things, but never have I seen such a knife."

Hesitantly, the man took the knife from Radan's hand and examined it. He called to the other boatmen and they hurried over to join him. Each took the knife in turn and looked closely at it.

Addressing the crowd, the boatman raised his voice to say, "We will need to use two boats to take you all across."

"When do we leave?" asked Izar.

"It is too late for us to go today. Tonight, we will find sleeping places for you in the village. If the weather is good tomorrow, then we will leave after morning food."

There was a buzz of excited conversation amongst the group, though many were clearly very nervous. This was obvious later when some of them examined the boats closely to gain confidence that these small craft really could be trusted to carry them across the wide sea. The fact that the wind had increased since they had arrived and the waves were larger and now capped with white foam, did nothing to ease their worry.

Before Izar went to his sleeping place that evening, he took out the one remaining knife he had and the last two of the three copper discs he had once made for his previous master, but never finished. He hid these in the bottom of his quiver where they were safe from Radan's demands.

Next morning, there was relief amongst the villagers when the boatmen decided that the state of the sea was too dangerous to make the crossing.

Unsaid, but accepted by all, by virtue of the mystical power he possessed, the Rhetian villagers regarded Izar as their leader. It was he who now called them together.

"We have survived a long journey, though it was not without loss. Now is the time of the longest days and we should speak to the Sun Spirit according to our way."

There was some hubbub amongst those gathered.

"Go collect your beakers, we must drink together."

Izar recalled old Rab's words, many years ago. He would use them, but unlike the ritual then, today they only had water to drink. When the villagers returned, they scooped up water from a small brook running past the settlement and Izar incanted, "The Sun Spirit reaches its zenith today as it did for our fathers, our fathers' fathers and those before. We pray for a new, young sun after the cold and darkness of the frozen time to come."

He held his beaker up as high as he could reach, and the crowd did the same. They all turned to the sun and drank of the liquid. Then Izar filled his beaker again. He turned to face inland, and as he poured the water over the ground he chanted, "Oh, Spirit of the earth and mountain, all good things come from you, here, take back some of your own."

Turning to the little crowd, he said, "Now, before we journey over the sea, it is the time of year to mark your hands."

Later, as he watched Tan struggling against the firm grip of those holding him, in a fruitless attempt to avoid the bone needle making a fifth dot on his hand, Izar reflected sadly on the fact that his decision to make this journey had shortened Rin's life and robbed his son of a mother. He himself now had three whole rows of dots on one hand and two on the other. He stared at his hands and stretched his fingers. He knew that no man could expect to live past having four complete rows of dots on each hand and he struggled to work out how many more summers he might see. His conclusion was that more than half of his life had gone; how would the last part of his life be? He was anxious about the voyage ahead of them, but excited that he might have the opportunity to use the gift Rab had given him.

The boatmen stood thigh deep in the sea, steadying the vessel as the passengers clambered, one by one, into the heavy craft. Each hesitated, waiting for the trough of a wave when the side of the boat was lower and then bundled themselves over the side and onto the deck. Yor helped Izar with one hand and held Tan with the other. When Izar was safely aboard, his friend passed the little boy to him. The two men seized each other's wrists and Izar called out, over the sound of the sea and the babble of passengers' voices, "Have a good life, my friend, I wish you wealth and success."

Radan, who was in the other boat, shouted to Yor, "May your child be born safely."

As far as he could in the confusion on the boat with the passengers trying to find a dry, comfortable place to sit, Izar watched Yor wading ashore. He was overcome by a deep sorrow at seeing the man who had helped him in so many ways, departing from his life forever. He suddenly felt very alone, even though he was in the middle of an uncomfortable crush of people. However, there was no time to dwell on his feelings.

As each of the two boats filled with people, the boatmen shouted instructions about where they should sit, to maintain the equilibrium of the vessels. They lifted up and down with the swell, making it clear to those aboard that they had lost contact with the land and now were at the mercy of sea, an element new and frightening for them. Finally, two boatmen climbed onto the bow and started paddling furiously to keep the boat heading out to sea. The other two gave a push and clambered onto the stern, where they too started to paddle as hard as they could. Not until they were well clear of the breakers did the men slow their strokes and start a rhythmic, coordinated paddling.

As a parent, Izar found courage in the totally strange and dangerous environment he now found himself in, by necessarily subduing fear in front of his son. At first, Tan was excited by the adventure, but as the boat drew out from the shore, his exultation was at first muted and then soon overcome by terror about the constant and rhythmic motion of the seemingly endless stretch of water around them.

"Must we stay in the boat?" he asked.

"Of course, the water is deep, and we are safe here," replied Izar.

He squeezed his son's hand. The boy moved closer to him.

"How long will it take before we can walk on the ground again?"

The father smiled at his son and those around him who had heard the question.

"Not long, you see how hard the men are paddling to take us across to the land over there," he said, pointing. He put his arm around the boy and hoped that the young one did not sense the anxiety his father felt.

As he held Tan tightly, he glanced down at him and tried to force from his mind the comparison he unwillingly made with another little boy, one who had given his life trying to assist the metal smith on his long journey. The memory of Lin's dreadful screams would always be with him.

The weather had improved greatly compared with the previous day and, apart from a breeze on the side of the vessel, the conditions were in their favour. Nevertheless, the beam wind tended to gust and occasionally gave an alarming push on the side, which, much to the distress of the passengers, rocked the boat. There were screams and shouts each time the boat tilted. However, what added to their unease was that sea water had begun to seep through the seams between the planks.

"Don't worry, water always comes in through the joints," shouted one of the boatmen in the stern when he noticed the passengers' discomfort. "Use the log to scoop the water and throw it overboard."

There were several hollow logs with one end closed lying on the deck. As the boat rolled, the water running across the floor lifted them and they floated around.

"Take Tan," said Izar as he passed the boy to a woman sitting next to him.

"We must do as the boatman tells us, take a log," he instructed men within reach of the containers. They needed no second bidding. The level of the water swilling around was making sitting on the deck uncomfortable as the passengers got increasingly wet.

"Must we do this all day?" complained one of the passengers.

The boatman laughed and replied, "It is much worse on rainy days."

The sun was high in the sky when Izar estimated that they were as far from the shore they had left as they were from their destination. They could now clearly see a row of white cliffs. But what worried him was that the current seemed to be pulling them sideways in the direction of the sun.

"Boatman, are we not to cross to the land with the white cliffs?"

"Yes, we are."

"But we are moving in a different direction."

"Fear not, Izar, for the current is now taking us that way, but today, when the sun starts to get lower, the sea will push us back to the way we wish to go."

The other boat was in sight and, although some distance away, it could be seen that passengers were busy scooping water from their deck too. This activity was now continuous on both boats. As the day progressed, the detail of the coast they were approaching became clearer. There was a row of high, steep, white cliffs and in the middle of them a hill that dominated the coast. There were several trails of smoke being blown by the wind. Obviously, there was a settlement of some sort on the high hill.

The travellers were beginning to believe that the boats really could get them safely to the far shore, but their confidence was shaken when the wind began to increase. The direction in which they were being paddled began to change and although the men on one side of the boat dipped their paddles into the sea fast and furiously to turn the vessel, it was obvious that the stiff breeze was determining where they would arrive on the coast in front of them. The passengers' anxiety increased too when some waves on the windward side began to slop over and onto the deck.

"Move over to the middle of the boat," instructed a boatman to those who were sitting on the side not being hit by the wind.

"Why?" asked one of them, not wishing to release a tight grip on the side of the hull.

"It is easier for us to paddle straight if the boat is balanced," the boatman replied.

There was a blast of wind and the boat lurched over.

"Move now, quickly. Do as I say!"

The passengers were near to desperation and quickly crept into the centre of the hull, grabbing whatever they could to steady themselves.

It was clear that they were being pushed sideways by the wind and the current as the boatmen furiously paddled towards the shore. The longer they were at sea drifting sideways, the further they would land from their intended destination. Gradually, the base of the cliff got closer and closer and the features of the beach became more distinct. Eventually, they rode through the swell. There was a cheer from the passengers when they heard the crunch as the bottom of the boat ground against the shingles on the shore. The four boatmen jumped over the side of the boat and started to drag it as far as possible up the beach. They steadied it as the travellers willingly jumped into the sea and waded ashore.

Izar tumbled over the side of the boat and only avoided being totally immersed by clinging on with one hand. The woman passed Tan to him and then clambered over herself. They both struggled up the incline to the shore as the relentless waves seemed to pursue them.

The boatmen pulled the craft further up the beach as soon as they had all disembarked. Some passengers collapsed onto the stony shore, rejoicing at having relatively secure ground under them after the insecurity of the wallowing boat.

"There is the other boat!" shouted Izar, pointing in the direction of the sun.

They stood up and watched as it was paddled through the surf some distance away. Unlike their landing on a flat shore, the other craft hit a rock and titled over, throwing out the passengers into the shallow sea. There were shouts of horror from those already ashore, some of whom ran, as far as was possible on loose shingle, to aid the others.

"Take Tan, woman, I'll go to the other boat," said Izar.

He hurried off as quickly as he was able, but as he neared the boat, it became clear that the victims of the capsized boat were plodding up the shingle, uninjured.

"So, you have arrived safely in the 'far country', Izar," said Radan as he waded ashore.

"Safely, but wet," he replied.

"Not as wet as we are."

"Where is the place that we will stay?" asked Izar.

"First, before the sun sets, we must go to the village on the high hill to ask for food and a place to sleep. Then, when the sun rises we will walk for five days in the direction of the setting sun."

Others heard what Radan said and there were calls of disbelief, "Five more days walking! "We have travelled enough," said one.

"Just five days and then you will arrive in a place, the like of which you have never seen. There will be huts for everyone and feasting to celebrate our arrival."

There were still some discontented mutterings, but Radan paid no attention.

CHAPTER 17

The travellers gathered up their belongings and walked along the beach. Izar struggled to keep up with the others, with his bag in one hand and Tan's hand in the other. The climb up the steep hill was very difficult for everyone, but most so for father and son. As they approached the village, Radan turned and said to the Rhetians, "The people who live here are from the tribe of the Regni."

Izar realised what would happen next, for he had seen it so many times during their journey: Radan and his warriors would terrorise the villagers into providing food and shelter for the group. However, he was wrong.

"Are the Regni people not friendly?" asked Izar.

"Usually, but they are wary of strangers. I will go to the village alone first to tell them who we are. I think they will welcome us," answered Radan.

"Why do you think so?"

"Because people in other tribes like to travel to the land of the Duran to attend rituals and see the sacred monuments. When I explain that I am the Duran Master's chief warrior, they will not dare to offend me."

The group sat on the grass and waited for Radan to return. A while later, they heard him calling to them from a distance and saw him beckoning with his arm that the group should move forward. When they met, he said, "It was as I thought, they are pleased to welcome me and my fellow travellers."

And so, the next day, their journey progressed, first through the territory of the Regni and then the Belgae. On the fifth day, as they followed a path through open hillside country, Radan announced, "We are now in the land of the Duran people, the people of my master."

"How much further do we have to travel?" asked Izar.

"We only need to get round the high ridge of hills in front of us and then you will see our village, Durotrin."

As the group walked around the edge of the ridge, the track turned. From their elevated position they suddenly had a view of a river and just beyond that an extraordinary sight. Though it was too distant to see any detail, it appeared that there were many rows of huts, some with smoke rising from them. Most of the huts were inside a huge, white circular shape that had been cut into the ground. To one side of the buildings was another, smaller circular shape. In it were what appeared to be many tall logs standing erect. The group stopped, mesmerised by the view.

"Move on, you can look at the village when you arrive," instructed Radan.

Sometime later they came to the bank of the wide river. The clear water was running in the direction of the midday sun.

"We must cross the river; you can see from here the avenue that leads to Durotrin."

"But the river is too deep for us to wade across," complained several of the Rhetians.

Radan paid no attention to them. He walked to the riverbank and shouted to men on the far side who were fishing. The fishermen pulled in their lines and ran to a row of log boats, which were pulled upon the land. Very soon they were paddling three boats towards the travellers.

The Rhetians had already got used to seeing the dark-haired people of the land they had been walking through since their voyage across the sea, but their appearance was novel to the fishermen who were to ferry them across the river. They stared with disbelief at the blond-haired, blue-eyed newcomers.

Radan could sense the travellers' discomfort and said, "The Duran people have never seen people such as you, pay them no attention. Come, climb onto the boats."

The fishermen had to make two trips to bring the whole group across the river. When they were all assembled, Radan led them along a very wide path towards what was, for the Rhetians, an unbelievable sight – huts, a huge number of them stretching as far as they could see. They were of a construction unknown to them. Instead of the simple wooden huts they were used to, these buildings were large and circular. Most had a pointed roof made of thick straw. The roofs reached the ground, though a few had a stone walls supporting them.

Radan and his men were greeted by Duran people as they walked along up a gentle slope, through the wide alley between the huts. Many of them stood gawping at the newcomers as they were led along. The warriors left them and dispersed, leaving the Rhetians with Radan.

"These are the homes of those who work on the monuments dedicated to our spirits, the gods of the sun and moon," Radan called out to the astounded Rhetians.

"Where are these monuments?" asked Izar.

"There is one here. Come, we will look at the Circle of the Sun," replied Radan, pointing at a gap between two huts.

The group filed through the gap and there before them was the entrance to a forest of logs.

"This is one of four gates to the circle, this one is the nearest to the noon day sun and the most holy of them."

The visitors gazed about them as they walked through the opening.

"But what are these logs for?" asked Izar.

"From these, our wise men determine many things, including when is the best time of year to plant our crops, when is the time for the celebration of the day the sun is highest and also the day that marks the middle of the cold season. Our feasting days are decided by when the shadow of certain trees coincide with particular places in the circle."

"Who are these wise men?" asked Izar.

"They are the ones with knowledge given to them by the Sun God. You may become one of them if you are successful and find favour with the master."

The group had been standing still while this conversation had been taking place.

"Come now, we must see the master," said Radan.

He led them quickly through the maze of logs to the far side of the circle. There they found three large huts in a row following the curve of the ditch. Outside of one there was a guard holding a spear. Radan approached the man and said something the others could not hear. He turned to the Rhetians and said, "We must wait here for the master to greet you."

The man with the spear pushed aside a large curtain made of the hide of an auroch, which covered the doorway of the hut, and entered. After a short while he returned and said something to Radan. He turned and said to the visitors, "The leader of our people will see us shortly."

"Who lives in the other big huts here?" asked Izar.

"These are the homes of the Wisemen. They are powerful and privileged. It is their knowledge, given to them by the Sun God, which bestows on them rights beyond those of ordinary men."

"Where will we live?" asked Izar.

"You will be given a hut and a woman to care for you and your son."

"Why is your leader so generous?"

"He will have high expectation of what you and your people can do. If you fail him, your time here will be short. Now, I believe that you have a gift for him."

Izar thought for a moment and then remembered where he had hidden the copper objects. He took the quiver off his belt and, holding the arrows, tipped it up and recovered the goods.

"Give him the best example of your work," Radan instructed him.

"I have a copper image of the sun that can be used as a necklace, quite like the one you have."

"That would be good, the sun is the most important thing in Duran beliefs," answered Radan.

Izar picked out the copper disc and started to polish it against his shirt as he awaited an audience with his new employer.

CHAPTER 18

The curtain on the door frame parted and a man appeared. He was of medium height with grey hair and beard. Izar judged that he was well past middle age and the crows' feet at the corner of his eyes and the furrows in his brow seemed to confirm this. He was wearing a long, woollen shirt gathered at the waist by a multicoloured sash. In his hands he was holding a headdress, as the height of the doorway had prevented him from putting it on until he got outside. It was the skull of a deer, the front of which had been removed so that it could be placed on his head. The antlers remained on the skull. Hanging from the back of the skull were long, thin coloured strips of leather. He flicked the leather tails so that they hung over his back and placed the skull on his head. The headdress made him look much taller and gave him a sinister air. Two other men appeared through the doorway and stood behind their master.

He nodded to Radan, smiled, seized his wrist and said something that seemed to be a question, for Radan quickly answered him. The man with the headdress slowly ran his eyes over the group of people in front of him, betraying no emotion. Then he turned to Radan and once more spoke to him. Radan stepped over to where Izar was standing and pointed at him while at the same time he spoke to the master. The man smiled again and raised a hand in greeting. Izar moved forward and handed the shining copper pendant to him. The man took it and examined it carefully before his wizened face turned to Izar and beamed with a smile. He then continued his conversation with Radan.

At length, Radan turned to the group and said, "The master bids you all welcome and thanks you for this gift. He looks forward to seeing what your knowledge can bring to his territory. He has had some huts built near here where you will form a colony of those gifted with the magic of the changing the nature of rocks."

When Radan stopped talking, the master beckoned to the two men behind him. They stepped forward and raised their right hands in greeting. They then indicated to the group to follow them.

"These men will show you to your huts," said Radan. "Izar, have one of the women take Tan with them. You should stay here."

After the group had left, the master beckoned the Rhetian to follow him into his hut, having first removed his headdress. Inside, the only light was that from the fire in the centre of the room. The master sat on a bench, which was probably his sleeping place, and indicated to the others to sit on the floor. He spoke at length with Radan, who from time to time answered him. Izar was able to follow part of the conversation, though he thought it best not to say so. Eventually, Radan turned to him.

"The master is pleased that you agreed to come to bring your mystical skills to Durotrin. He wishes that you start your work as soon as possible."

"But it will take some time to make the necessary arrangements," said Izar.

"What arrangements?" asked Radan.

"We must build special fires, ovens where we can burn wood to make the material that will give extreme heat for our processes."

The master interrupted Izar, asking Radan a question. After a short conversation Radan turned to Izar and said, "The master says that you will have all the labour you need to prepare for your work. What else must you have?"

"We will need a constant supply of logs to burn in our ovens. We must have a covered place to make casts and also a place to finish and polish the copper."

"You will have all these things."

"Oh, yes of course there is the most important thing," said Izar.

"What is that?"

"We need to find a supply of rocks that are of a kind only I can recognise."

Radan turned back to the master and spoke with him for some time before he looked at Izar and said, "The master will have rocks brought to you from different places in the land of the Duran people. There must surely be some with the properties you require."

The master spoke again and, although Izar had understood most of what had been said, Radan once more translated, "The master says that to celebrate your safe arrival after the long journey, tomorrow we will have a pig feast."

"A pig feast?"

"Yes, the food we have when we celebrate is the meat of pigs.".

The audience was over, and the men left the hut.

"Come, I'll show you where you are to live," said Radan.

"Is my son in the same place?" asked Izar.

"Yes, he will be with your woman. She is called Fer."

They walked back along the pathway, through the forest of standing logs. Izar had more time to consider how they had been laid out. Many were positioned in huge rings, with great accuracy, equidistant from each other. There was also a group of logs in the centre of the smallest ring where each was spaced in an elaborate pattern.

The next day, when the sun was at its full height, Radan called to see Izar.

"Leave Tan with your woman and come with me, we have much to do. I have brought a donkey for you ride."

"It is difficult for the boy for the woman does not speak the way of the Rhetian," answered Izar.

"He will quickly learn the Duran way of speaking. Come, we must decide where we shall build the fireplaces you need."

The two men found their way out of the village in the direction of the midday sun, following a wide path leading up a hill.

"What is that place?" asked Izar excitedly while pointing at a similar scene to that of the mighty earthworks and logs adjacent to the village they had just left. "The circular earth wall and ditch is just like the one in Durotrin."

"Come, we can look at the holy place of the Sun God," answered Radan.

The entrance was through an opening in the earthen wall, which was wide enough for four men side by side to enter. The opening faced the direction from which they had come, the direction of the rising summer sun.

When they entered the massive construction, it became apparent that the thick logs were in rings. The huge logs, while less numerous than those at the other site, were equally impressive.

"There are six rings, each has another ring within, except for the final ring, which surrounds the altar. The logs that make the rings are spread an equal distance apart from each other,." explained Radan.

"Why do the Duran have these rings?" asked Izar.

"In our beliefs the ring, in some form, is the most important shape. It is that of life making a full transit from earth to birth, ascending to adulthood, old age and then declining to eventual return to the soil, the earth where life began."

"And you communicate with the spirit of the sun here?"

"Yes, this is the place of sacrifice. Here we give offering to the spirit so that we will be favoured. The sacrifices are usually made before the warm time, to ask for a good harvest, and at the beginning of the dark time, to ask for good health through the cold season and new light after the dark time."

They wandered through the posts until they came to the open space in the centre. In the middle was a huge, flat stone, half the height of a man.

"You see the blood on the stone, the blood of many children who have been honoured to die here to appease the spirit."

The Rhetian looked at the altar with some disbelief.

"Children?"

"Yes, for only children are pure enough to please the spirit," said Radan.

"How old are these children?" asked Izar.

"Up to five years old, sometimes six. After that age children are not considered to be pure."

"And the parents permit this?"

"Yes, for it is a great honour to give your child to the Sun God. If you are fortunate, the wise men might choose Tan, for he is a very special child with golden hair and blue eyes."

Izar felt a slight tremble as he gazed at the blood-stained alter stone.

"Come, the sun is getting lower, we have more to see," said Radan.

The two men left the site and walked through some trees along a path leading down the hill. When they came to a clearing, they saw the river they had been ferried across the day before. After a short while they came to a wide track crossing their path. The track led down to the riverbank.

"This is the place where I think you could do your work," stated Radan.

"Why do you say so?" asked Izar.

"There are several reasons. This track continues for a very long distance from the direction where the sun sets, to the place where it rises, and crosses the river here. You see that the water divides into smaller streams shallow enough to wade across. Yet just a little further up, the river is so deep that a boat can float. This would allow you to have timber for your fires transported either by boat from far away past Durotrin where there are mighty forests, or along the track from the forests we have seen on our journey. There is another reason – here there is no danger of you causing the village to burn."

"But we would be some distance from our huts," said Izar.

"The master will build new homes for you and your workers here."

"Good, then we will build our work place here," stated Izar.

"It shall be done, but now we must return to Durotrin, for at sunset we are to have the pig feast," said Radan.

As he spoke, they became aware of a swelling sound: the deep roar of many voices from beyond the bushes beside the track.

"What's that noise?" Izar asked.

"Ah, the men are returning from their work. They are finishing early today to enjoy the feast."

The two of them stood and watched as a long column of men emerged from the cover of the bushes and marched along the track towards them. A large plume of dust, raised by many, many feet, was rising from the dry earth of the well-worn trail.

As the procession moved past them, Izar could see that many carried picks, stout ash staves with parts of antlers bound to them.

Raising his voice to be heard, Izar said to Radan, "What work are they doing?"

"They are fulfilling the Wisemen's plan to change the place of the dead."

"The place of the dead?"

"It is the most sacred place in our culture. What you have seen here so far is the place of the Sun God and the holy circles of Durotrin. The great works in these places are made of wood. The logs will eventually decay, but the place of the dead, the place where purified bodies enter the afterlife, will never decay, for it is made of stone."

Neither spoke for a long time as they watched the weary workmen tramp past. Eventually, at the end of the long column, came women carrying baskets and several donkeys pulling carts with wooden water containers.

"This place, the place of the dead, can I see it?" asked Izar.

"Yes, but we must hurry so that we can return to the village in time for the feast."

Izar turned the donkey and they set off. Radan took the leading rope to try to get the animal to speed up.

After a while, as they emerged from the cover of trackside bushes, from his vantage point on top of the donkey, Izar was the first to see the astounding sight of the massive white blocks of stone in the distance. The circle of monoliths was surrounded by an equally white chalk embankment.

"By the gods, this is extraordinary!" said the Rhetian.

"You are impressed?"

"Yes, mightily so," retorted Izar.

"Wait until we get closer, then you will see how big the stones are."

As they neared the site, they passed two enormous, grey stones lying on rafts of logs. The long lines of ropes laying on the ground had obviously been used to drag the rocks on the rolling timbers.

Izar was shocked into silence by the magnificence of the stone structure. As he rode closer, he could not but admire the incredible engineering feat. When they approached the site, it became apparent that the five enormous standing stones were placed in the shape of a horseshoe with the opening in the direction where the sun rose. On top of them, linking them together, they were capped by stones placed horizontally. Around these monsters there was a line of smaller stones that had been polished, betraying a blue hue. Beyond these stones there were a number of standing stones forming an outside circle, but this line was incomplete. Izar counted them and saw that there were as many as the dots on two hands and two more.

"As you see," said Radan, "the men are working on the outside circle. When they are finished, there will as many as you have fingers, three times over. The tops of these will be linked with stones capping them."

"These outside stones are grey, the big ones in the middle are white."

"Yes, the builders will scrape the stones when they are finished to make them the same colour as the others."

Izar climbed off the donkey and walked around the stones. It was obvious where the men had been working. Lines scratched on the ground showed where holes were to be dug for the missing stones. In some places the digging was well advanced. One large stone was outside of the circle waiting to be erected.

"The stone you see lying there is to be stood up in this hole," said Radan, pointing at a gaping gap in the ground.

"But how do you lift them?" said an astonished Izar.

"This is the secret of the Duran people. The chief builders have the knowledge to raise the stones. They direct the work."

"And this is the place of the dead?"

"Yes, you can see the graves there around the outside of the circle. The bones of our most important forefathers lie there, and one day mine will too."

"But you don't bury the bodies?"

"No, the dead are burned to purify them before they meet the Earth God."

"And only the bones are buried? No goods for the journey to the next world?"

"No, that is not our way. The Earth God will provide for the spirits of our people."

As they talked, several young children were running around the standing stones. Their tattered clothing was covered in chalk dust, as were their faces and hair.

"The children show no respect for this place," said Izar.

Radan laughed and said, "No, but I am surprised they have energy to play, for they work here all day, every day."

Radan noticed the surprise on Izar's face.

"They work every day?" he asked.

"Oh yes, they help to dig the holes."

"Why?" asked Izar, in a surprised tone.

"You can see, the holes are too small for two men to work in, but several children can. And the pits have to be very deep, men could not work down there," Radan said, pointing into the hole.

"How can they be forced to work?"

"If they don't work, they don't eat."

"Whose children are they?"

"No one's. They are children with no parents, or with parents who don't want them."

"Where do they live?"

"Over there in those huts," said Radan, nodding towards some poorly built shelters. "Come, stand in the middle of the circle."

Both men made their way into the middle.

"You see that standing stone over there?" asked Radan, pointing at a large rock, the height of two men, outside the circle.

"Yes," said Izar.

"On the day in the middle of the warm time, if you stand here, the sun will rise exactly behind it. And if you look this way," said Radan, turning round, "when the sun sets on the day in the middle of the cold time you will see it through this arch of the biggest standing stones, and the arch of two on the outside of the circle."

"I find it difficult to understand these things you tell, how can they be known to you?"

Radan laughed, "These are things the Wisemen and the Wisemen before them and those even before, have learned and shown the builders where to place the stones. But come, we must hurry, or we will be late for the feast."

As they made their way back to the village, the Rhetian quizzed Radan about the beliefs of the Duran people and the holy places. He marvelled at the sheer effort that his hosts invested in such enormous enterprises, but he was perplexed that he could not comprehend the necessity for it.

CHAPTER 19

As they approached Durotrin, it was apparent from the pillars of smoke that cooking fires were burning inside the broad, earthen walls surrounding it. The sound of many, many voices filled the air. There was some chanting, much laughter and the shrill sound of pigs protesting about being dragged into the village. Judging by the smell of cooking that filled the air, some had already been slaughtered.

"Come, we must tell the master of our decision about the site for your work. He will be with the Wisemen at their cooking place away from all the crowds," shouted Radan, trying to make himself heard over the noise.

Izar stopped and climbed off the donkey. "I must go to Tan to see if he is happy with my woman. I can take him with us."

No sooner had he said this, than he realised that it might be unwise to draw the attention of the Wisemen to the blue eyed, fair-haired young boy. The sight of the blood on the altar stone was fresh in his mind.

He quickly re-joined Radan, who was some steps ahead and walked with him along the path towards the master's hut.

Although much of the circle was crowded, there was an area in front of the hut where there were only a few people.

Those who were there had clustered around the cooks, busy with the roasting of a pig over a large fire.

As Izar and Radan approached, a knot of people who were talking together broke up and turned their attention to them. Izar recognised the master. He was once more wearing the deer's head, though now he was dressed in a fine fur coat. On the front of it, hanging from a leather thong, was the copper pendant. The master came towards the two men, leaving the couple, who Izar assumed must be the Wisemen, and shouted a greeting. Radan responded and started to talk to the master. Izar understood some parts of the conversation and realised that he was telling the chieftain about the place the metal smith had chosen for his work. Izar noticed the Wisemen casting glances at him and making comments to each other. He could not hear the conversation, but the sight of them made him feel uneasy. The Wisemen also had headdresses. One had the skin of a wolf draped around his shoulders and the skull of the wolf, with bared teeth, on his head. The other was dressed in a similar fashion, though in his case it was the head and fur of a bear.

The master looked well pleased, for he frequently smiled as Radan spoke to him. At length he looked at Izar and said something that Radan translated as, "You have chosen a good place. When the sun rises tomorrow, my builders will begin to prepare the workplace for you and build you a hut."

"Please tell the master that I am grateful and wish to begin my work as soon as I can."

Radan translated what Izar had said. He then turned and said, "The master has sent out a message for samples of the rocks from different areas in his lands to be brought for you to see."

The wizened old man beckoned to Izar to follow him. He led him over to where the Wisemen were standing. Radan followed. Izar raised a hand in greeting, to which they responded in the same way, though in a half-hearted fashion. The Wisemen's faces were partly obscured by their headdresses, but as far as he could see they were younger than the master. He looked at their hands, but the Duran did not have dots on their hands the same way he did, so there was no way of telling their age. Neither of them smiled, but with piercing eyes, surveyed him from head to toe. The master spoke to them, pointing at Izar, but the two men did not seem impressed.

"They don't seem to like me," Izar whispered to Radan.

"They see you as a threat, for they are the all-knowing, all-seeing spiritual leaders of the tribe, and they recognise that you have knowledge they do not. Thus you have power to rival them."

This comment sounded ominous. Izar asked Radan, "But then why did the master wish us to come to Durotrin?"

"The master is a man of vision and enterprise. It needs a man like him to maintain and improve the monuments you have seen today. Part of his vision is for the Duran people to increase their knowledge. Making things from molten stone is an important part of that," replied Radan.

"So, there is conflict between the master and the Wisemen," said Izar.

"There is no conflict, the master decides what is best for his people."

Izar thought it best not to pursue the subject further, but he was perturbed about the apparent hostility of the Wisemen.

The silence was broken by one of the pair asking Radan a question. He turned to Izar and said, "They want to know when you will perform your magic with the stone."

"Tell them that we must first find the right kind of stone. We also need to build fires to create great heat to produce the alchemy."

Radan translated Izar's reply and then they responded by seemingly asking another question.

"They ask what you do to pacify the Spirit of the Earth when you steal stone from the ground," said Radan on their behalf.

"Tell them that it is our belief that everything we take from the earth should be replaced. We return the broken stone to the holes we made in mining it. We only retain a small amount of the rocks. Eventually, we repay the debt by burying our own bodies in ground, which has supported our lives and given us meat and fruit."

When Radan reported this answer to the Wisemen, there was some disturbance. They raised their voices at him. He was somewhat flustered when he turned to Izar and said, "They do not like the thought that you bury the bodies of the dead impurified by fire. It is our way to cleanse a body with fire before the bones are buried."

As he was talking, one of the Wisemen shouted something at him. Clearly, there was something he wanted Radan to add to his reply.

"What did he say?" asked Izar.

"Don't worry, it's not important."

"Please tell me, what was it he was angry about?"

Radan hesitated and Izar pleaded once more. At length, he said, "The Wisemen insist that if you take stone from the ground, you must sacrifice to the Earth Spirit to give thanks."

There was a silence for a few moments and some awkwardness before Radan added, "Come, come and eat."

He turned to the Wisemen and the master and respectfully nodded to them, before shepherding Izar towards the blazing hearth where the pig was being turned on a spit. There, gathered around the fire were their travelling companions, the Rhetiains.

Izar called out, "How are you all?".

Several responded at the same time, but their smiling faces indicated that they were happy in their new circumstances, and Izar's fears that there might be some discontent were allayed.

"We have good huts and they bring us more food than we can eat," said one.

"This is a wonderous place, though we cannot understand the importance of all the tall logs," said another.

Radan addressed the whole group when he called out to them, "The beliefs of the Duran are different from yours, but you will learn of them and soon understand."

What Radan had not noticed was that the master had sauntered towards the cooking hearth, following them. He too wanted to appraise the feelings of the visitors.

"But why do you make such huge structures? Why is it necessary?" asked one man.

Just as Radan was about to reply, the master made himself known by asking him what the Rhetians wanted to know. Radan translated the question.

The master held up his hand to greet the newcomers and started to speak to them. After each sentence, Radan interpreted what he had said.

"There are two important things you should know, the most holy shape is the circle. It represents the cycle of the seasons of the year, from the cold time to the growing time, from the hot time through the time of plenty with the harvest and then, as the year dies, back to the cold time. It has other significance too, there is the cycle of our lives. The Earth God gives us life and we follow a cycle through childhood, manhood, old age and death. At the end our bones are purified and returned to the Earth God from whence they came. The circle is completed when new life springs from the earth."

There was a stunned silence for a while. None of them had heard Radan ever talk of the beliefs and customs of the Duran. The master's speech rankled with some as they realised that his attitude showed that he considered the beliefs of the Duran to be superior to those of the Rhetians.

The silence was broken by the voice of a woman, who shouted, "You said that there were two important things!"

"What did she ask?" said the master to Radan. He translated the question. The master was silent for a while, considering his answer. Then he spoke through the interpreter.

"Yes, there is another important thing, something you must appreciate if you are to live here."

He turned his head from side to side, surveying the group in front of him, making eye contact with those who dared to look directly at him.

"The Duran are a great people and we have a closeness to our gods that is denied to others. We earn this privilege by impressing the spirits. We make ever greater symbols of the holy circles to demonstrate our recognition of them."

He pointed to the mighty logs behind them and then continued. "These are a sign of our dedication to pleasing our gods, but there are more great works, many more and the greatest of them is not made with wood, which can decay and corrupt, but with stone, colossal rocks that require more men than there are hairs on a dog's back to transport and erect. You will see them and you will marvel at the superior power and ingenuity of the Duran."

When the last sentence of the speech was delivered to the group there was a long, awkward silence, but the master did not wait for a reaction. He turned and, without comment, started walking back towards where the Wisemen were still standing.

Izar sensed that the Rhetians were disturbed by what they had heard. At length, he held up his hands and shouted, "Listen, hear me. I have news. Tomorrow we will start to prepare our place of work, the place where we will show that our people, those who live in the land where we have come from, also have power and ingenuity, for we will turn stone into copper. Only we have the knowledge to do so and that is why the Duran have asked us to come here."

There were shouts of assent and some smiles. Radan said nothing.

CHAPTER 20

The master was true to his word, for when Izar and Tan, together with some of the other Rhetians, approached the site that had been selected, there were men swarming all over the area. One group was hacking at the undergrowth with deer antlers, which had been given a sharp edge, another was felling saplings with stone axes, their action producing a chorus of thudding sounds. Behind those who were doing the clearance was another group of men levelling the ground, using cow-bone shoulder blades as shovels.

"Why have you chosen this place? It's far from the village," said one of the Rhetian men.

"We need plenty of wood for our fires, here the tracks from the forests cross the river. The logs can be transported by cart or by boat," responded Izar.

"And the same is true for the rocks you will need," said a voice from behind them.

It was Radan, who had just arrived from the village. He motioned to Izar to step aside so that he could talk to him in private.

"The master wishes to see you. He has received good news from a runner with a message."

"What news?" asked Izar.

"He would not tell me, come let's hurry."

On their way back to the village, they passed a long file of men, some carrying wooden and bone shovels and others antler picks. They were making their way towards the stone ritual site that Radan had shown Izar the day before. Further on, the pair passed through the rows of huts and into the circle of standing logs. Men were working inside the circle, digging a great hole near to the posts. The Wisemen were using a long rawhide rope, one at each end, to determine exactly where a felled tree with its branches cut off, which was lying on the ground, should be erected. Normally, Izar would have been inclined to stop to watch, but his desire to know what news the master had, overcame his natural curiosity. The Wisemen looked at them as they passed; Izar nodded his head at them as a sign of recognition, but the pair did not condescend to making a greeting.

When they arrived at the big hut, they saw the master standing outside, next to a tall youth. He left the boy, greeted Izar and ushered them inside. He told the two men to sit by the hearth, while he remained standing.

Out of respect, Izar and Radan waited for the old man to begin the conversation.

"I have waited for many full moons for the return of Radan with a knowledgeable one such as you."

There was a pause while he gathered his thoughts.

"While Radan was away, traders from the Silurian tribe visited me to make an exchange of goods, as they do every warm season. I told them that one with the gift of changing stone into another form would soon be coming to Durotrin and that he would perform such mysticism here."

Izar could contain his inquisitiveness no longer.

"Where is the land of the Silurians?"

The master was not used to being interrupted, and he took a deep breath to indicate some irritation, but acquiesced to the younger man.

"The Silurians are mountain people. Their land is far away, in the direction of the warm season setting sun."

"How far distant?" asked Izar.

"It takes two full moons to walk there, for there are many high mountains on the way and a wide river."

Radan turned to Izar and shook his head a little to try to indicate to the Rhetian that he was not expected to ask questions unless invited to do so.

"The traders knew of the matter of making metal, though they had never seen it. But what they had seen on their journey to our land was a place where men broke the special rocks from a hole in the mountain. They had made a passage deep into the ground."

"Did they describe these rocks?" asked Izar.

"No, but they described how the workers broke the rocks into small pieces and washed them in a stream before they were packed into wicker creel baskets to be transported by donkey to a place where the magic would be performed."

"Where is this place?"

"They didn't know. I told them that I would pay a great price if they could get me such rocks so that when Radan returned we might use them."

Izar was now very excited and blurted out, "But will they do so?"

"Yes, yes this is the news I have. The traders sent a runner, you saw him outside. He tells me that they are on their way here with many baskets of the stones you require."

Radan now threw caution to the wind and asked, "When will they arrive?"

The master did not answer; instead, he walked across to the entrance of the hut where the door hurdle was still open and called out to the boy to come join them.

The lad showed great respect to the master, bowing as he came in.

"Tell them of your journey to get here," he said as he pointed at the two men.

"Master, it was long and dangerous. We filled the baskets with the stones from the mine works and put them on our donkeys, one basket on each side. Several animals died on the way through the mountains, they slipped and fell on the wet rocks, others collapsed from exhaustion."

Izar interrupted the speaker, asking, "How many baskets will be left when they arrive here?"

The youth paused, looked at his fingers and held up both hands.

"As many as my fingers. We started the journey with as many fingers as that of two men, but the losses I told you of were added to when we reached the great river, for there three of the animals were swept away by the spirit of the river who was angered by us trespassing on his waters."

The master spoke, "And those who are left, when will they arrive in Durotrin?"

"In two or three days I think."

Clearly, the meeting was over as the master looked at the two men and pointed towards the door. This was just as well, as Izar had had difficulty in holding his tongue to express the severe misgivings he was feeling.

As they walked back towards where the workplace was being prepared, he unburdened himself to Radan.

"We will need more rocks than these Silurians are bringing, much more if we are to have enough copper to make Durotrin famous for its metal working."

"As you heard, the journey is hazardous."

"But they must make many journeys to supply our wants."

Radan was becoming exasperated by Izar's demands and answered, "The cost of transporting the rocks will be very high. You will have to be content with what the traders are bringing."

"That I will not, I have travelled through wet and cold and every imaginable danger to offer my skills to your master. I cannot achieve his ambition to make Durotrin a great metal centre if I cannot get the materials I need."

"Your demands already cause the master huge costs. The transport from the land of the Silurians is difficult and dangerous. We know this because many of our forefathers died dragging the blue stones you saw in the Place of Death, from the Silurian mountains."

"Is this true?"

"Yes, it is so."

There was a pause and then Radan's ruthlessness was once more apparent when he added, "There are those who greatly resent the Master's wealth being squandered on these new ideas you bring, when we have more important work building the ritual places. I have kept you alive for many full moons, but only to serve my master. Now others are urging me to serve them and remove what they see as a scourge that distracts our leader."

Izar grasped the meaning of the veiled threat. It was not difficult for him to understand who these "others" were.

And so developed an increasingly vitriolic relationship between the Rhetian metal workers and a faction led by the Wisemen. In the middle, the master tried to juggle between the newcomers' increasing demands for resources and those traditionally required to be dedicated to works honouring and appeasing the gods. The irregular and increasingly meagre supply of rocks from the land of the Silurians caused long periods when the hearth in the workshop was cold, there being no rocks to heat. Discontent grew amongst the Rhetians who, without work, were forced to join the labourers in dragging huge stone monoliths to the new ritual place. A cold time came and went and then a second. After the mid-summer ritual, Tan had markings on all of one hand and two fingers on the other. His father now had an increasing concern for the legacy of metal working he had hoped to pass on to his son.

However, two things happened during this period that gave Izar some hope for the future.

CHAPTER 21

Izar was still confounded by the criticism Zef had made of his casting method. He lay awake many a night considering the process that he was never allowed to see demonstrated. It was towards the end of the first cold time the Rhetians spent in Durotrin that he solved the mystery.

"Come, Tan, closer to the hearth. It will warm you."

The boy was shivering.

"No small wonder you are cold, throw away the icicle in your hand."

The boy was not of a mind to give up his plaything and looked for something to wrap around the ice so that it did not draw the heat from his hand. His eye fell on the clay rolled out on the work bench. He took a piece and wrapped it around the cold ice. Izar looked on, mildly irritated, but as always, very tolerant of his motherless child.

"Come, do as I say. Sit near me, here on the log."

Izar opened his cloak and covered the boy.

"See, Father, the ice is melting in the heat."

They both watched as the drips of water from the funnel, formed by the clay wrapped round the icicle, fell into the edge of the hearth and hissed as they disappeared.

"What will be left when the ice has disappeared, Father?"

"Only the clay, Tan. Though it is getting very soft."

There was a silence, father and son enjoying each other's company. Suddenly, Izar stood up, dropping the cloak on the ground. Tan was startled as his father shouted, "That's it, this is the way Zef uses the beeswax!."

Tan was shocked, afraid that his father was angry with him, and stuttered, "But, what do you mean, why are you shouting?"

Izar, had his hands to his face, fingers covering his eyes as he lamented, "How stupid of me. Tan, your father is beyond stupidity. Come, we must go to the village to find beeswax."

Though there was a shortage of copper, Izar spent days and weeks perfecting a new process. First, he sculpted the blade of a knife in beeswax, then covered the form with several layers of clay. This was the easy part. The real challenge was to bake the clay at such a temperature that when the melted beeswax ran out, the clay was hard enough that it did not collapse into the void formed. When he finally perfected this, the drained beeswax left a mould with the true shape of the knife he had sculpted. Finally, came the casting. Several of the Rhetians assisted as he gingerly poured the molten copper into the mould and it took the place of the displaced beeswax.

"When the copper has cooled, we will see if the method improves our work," he said to the onlookers.

They waited uneasily, giving the mould time to cool.

"Come Tan, watch as we break the mould."

Izar lifted the boy up onto the work bench.

"Here, use this small hammer to break it," said Izar as he handed him the deer bone.

The boy tapped gently.

"Harder, hard as you can."

The hammer descended on the clay and a large crack appeared.

"Stop, let me peel off the pieces."

Soon they had before them a perfectly formed replica of the beeswax blade.

Izar was quick to show the master the improved quality of his casting. He needed to continuously seek to strengthen his case for more copper, but the truth was that the metal workers' demands were sapping the wealth of community.

In the second warm season of the Rhetians' stay in Durotrin, the traders arrived with such rocks as they could supply, an amount that was once more a disappointment to Izar. By this time, the Silurians were aware that the difficulty of supplying the heavy material was causing some friction with their trading partner. In order to improve relations, they brought a gift for the master.

Izar watched as the traders unwrapped a hare skin package. One man was holding it and another carefully pulled back layers of pelt. When the last piece was removed, those craning their necks to view the present were confronted by four gnarled, differing shaped objects, about the size of a man's thumb. They glinted weakly in the sunshine.

"Izar, is this copper?" asked the master.

Izar leaned forward to inspect the objects, then he picked one up.

"It feels heavier than a piece of copper that size would do, and the colour is different."

One of the traders said, "Some of our landsmen found these in the bed of a stream, among the stones. We have heard stories that such as these can be transformed into objects of beauty."

"Do you know how?" asked the master.

"No, such knowledge is held by wise ones we have met."

"Can you make these into precious things, Izar?"

"I have no doubt that these are some form of metal, but not such as I have seen or heard of."

"Then they are of no value to me."

The master was gravely disappointed with the traders' gift and pushed it back towards the men who had presented it.

"No, no wait. I must learn to understand the nature of this metal. Let me try to use it," urged Izar.

The master took the pieces back and passed them to Izar. He left the crowd examining the objects as he walked off in the direction of the workshop.

The new material proved to be a distraction for the Rhetian from his primary activity, a distraction he needed, for the lack of copper-bearing rocks was proving to be limiting his ambition to create a centre of great importance. He knew that it would not be long before the master would become disillusioned with his efforts. Izar reached a decision on what was to be done, but before he announced it to the master, he spent time experimenting with the metal nuggets. He found that the metal could be scratched and also that it changed shape when beaten with a rock. However, when he tried to melt one of the pieces in his hearth, he was disappointed that, unlike copper, it showed no ability to change its form into liquid metal.

Finally, he decided that he should report his findings to the master, but he feared that his failure to use the material would make it even more likely that the man's confidence in him would suffer. He needed to give the old man some good news.

As he made his way to the master's hut, through the throng of workers erecting new logs in the great circle, he was conscious of the malign looks he was getting from many of them and in particular the Wisemen. He could make out some mutterings about the privileged position the Rhetian enjoyed. This animosity had been growing for some time, doubtless because of resentment regarding the resources lavished on his work, but also because he was seen to represent what was perceived to be a threat to change their way of life. He knew too that his disability brought him some disdain.

"Master, I tried to use the metal the traders brought, but so far I have had no success."

The man glowered at his visitor and very slowly and deliberately said, "You only bring me bad news and complaints."

"Master, I am aware that you have been very generous to me and my people, but we have not served you as well as we wished. The supply of the rocks I need is difficult and expensive for you. I wish to propose a solution."

"It is true. To transport the stones over the Silurian mountains and across the great river takes a long time and consumes my resources. There are those who would have me cease my attempt to bring progress and change to this community. Indeed, their complaints are hard to resist. What is your proposal?"

"I have a good friend who travelled with us across the mountains and forests on our journey here. He stayed on the other side of the great sea."

Impatiently, the master interrupted. "What purpose can this friendship serve?"

"He works with copper, but he does not make it from rocks. His master buys the copper from far away in the direction of the midday sun."

"How would this help us?"

"It is much easier to transport copper for our needs than to carry the rocks. For every basket of rocks yields a very small amount of copper. We could trade with my friend to get the metal."

"But how would you bring it here?"

"We could transport enough on one donkey to serve our need for half of the time from one warm season to another."

The master scratched his beard and pondered what he had heard.

"Come back when the sun rises tomorrow. I will discuss this with Radan."

The next morning Izar attended the master as instructed. He found that Radan was already there.

"I have decided that you will take goods to trade with your friend. Radan will accompany you. You must leave your son here as an assurance to me that you will return."

Izar was greatly perturbed by the master's condition. He had never been away from the boy. He realised though, that if he did not agree, then the master would be suspicious about his intentions.

After a short hesitation he said, "Then we should leave before the warm time finishes."

The conversation had left Izar in a state of torment. He was thrilled to have the chance to meet Yor again and to seek a way out of the dilemma regarding the supply of the raw material he needed, but the price he had to pay was high. He would have to entrust Tan to the keeping of Fer, the Duran woman he was living with. She seemed trustworthy and was good with the boy, but he and Radan could be away for perhaps two full moons. Would she take proper care of his son? The boy he loved so much. His decision about the journey was made. There was no alternative, but he would ask the Rhetian women to keep a close eye on Tan's welfare.

"Tan, I must go on a journey, a long journey."

"Can I come too, Father?

"I'm sorry, but that is not possible."

"But why not? We have been on a very long walk together before."

"Yes, but this time I can't take you. I will travel with Radan and we cannot take children. His boy can't go either."

"Who will give me food?"

"Fer will look after you."

"But she can't speak our way."

"You understand her when she calls you to eat!"

Izar leaned across and tousled the boy's hair.

"Please, Father."

Izar found it difficult to maintain the tender tone and the conversation ended by him telling Tan firmly that Fer would look after him and the Rhetian women would visit him every day. Nevertheless, he dreaded taking farewell of the boy and the likely emotional scene.

CHAPTER 22

The late summer sun was casting long shadows as it sank towards the horizon, an ill-defined line between the blue of the calm sea and the azure sky. The weary travellers wound their way through the small village until they came to the hut of Old Zef. It was not the old man himself who was in the open-sided workshop. A tall, well-built man, still in the prime of his life, looked up from the bench to see who was disturbing his concentration.

"Izar, Radan! Is it really you? What brings you back to our village?"

The two men clambered off the tired donkeys they had been riding and Radan pulled in the line attached to a third donkey, which was heavily laden. On a second line were two large dogs, their muzzles tied with a leather thong. Izar stretched to loosen muscles that had become cramped during the ride, and hobbled towards Yor. Both men threw their arms round each other.

"I am very happy to see you, Izar, you too, Radan."

As he spoke, two half naked children appeared through the doorway to the building, followed by their mother, a woman the visitors recognised as Yor's woman. The two men nodded to her in recognition. She smiled and then went back into the hut, calling the children to follow her.

"So, the baby you were expecting when we left, is a boy!" said Izar.

"And thanks to the Earth God that he was born safely and my woman survived," said Yor.

"Where is Zef?" asked Radan.

"He died soon after you went away. He gave me his hut and workshop."

"And you continue his work?" said Izar.

"Yes, and there is much work to do, for he made this village famous for making very good copper knives, decorations and objects of value. Many traders come here. But tell me, why have you come? You look like traders too."

"And that is what we are," said Izar. "We have fine furs and woven blankets. We have two hunting dogs left. We had three but we had to use one to trade for the boatmen to take us across the great sea."

"But why are you trading these things, are you not making copper?"

"Yes, we are, but very little. I had hoped to make my own copper, but there are no good rocks in the land of the Duran. I have decided to do like Zef did and buy raw copper from the land far away in the direction of the midday sun."

"This is the best way."

"So, we have come to you to ask if you can trade raw copper for us."

Yor started to laugh.

"Why do you laugh at me?" demanded Izar, who was feeling a sense of humiliation, having to ask the man who had once been his apprentice, to solve his problem.

"I am not laughing at you, I am just happy at the thought that after all you gave me, you taught me, you trusted me with your knowledge, now I can help you."

"Can you help us?" asked Izar with a tone that avoided expressing the desperation he felt.

"Yes, the men from the far land of which Zef spoke come here very often to trade. They have more copper than I need. Come, I will tell my woman to make food for us and we can talk."

"First we must water the donkeys and the dogs."

"Leave them, I will tell my girl to do this."

"She can tend the donkey, but I will see to the dogs, they are fearsome beasts."

Later, after they had eaten and exchanged news, Yor said, "It's getting dark, you can sleep in my hut, tomorrow I'll show you my work."

"Izar, you stay here, I have friends in the village. I'll stay with them until the traders come," said Radan.

"You can keep the animals here," said Yor.

That being agreed, Radan left.

The next morning the two men went to the workshop and Yor proudly showed Izar samples of his craft.

As he looked at the copper castings, Izar said, "I left before Zef showed you the secret of using the beeswax, but I have learned to use this method too to make knife blades."

"But I have made other things too, see here, look at this arrow head."

Izar took it and inspected it carefully.

"Have you tried to make an arrow using this?" he asked.

"No, but I'm sure that you would like to," said Yor enthusiastically. "Zef showed me something else that the copper can be used for," he said as he delved into a straw-lined, hollow log. He slowly pulled out a shining object, the like of which Izar had never seen or imagined.

He gazed in awe at the small bowl in Yor's hand. "Is this copper?" he stuttered.

"Yes, yes I am learning to make such drinking vessels, but it takes much time and often the process goes wrong."

"Copper is never wasted, you can melt it and use it again. But tell me, how could you make this?"

"You will recall that when we lived in the village where Radan found us, you made a disc. A disc that he forbade us to make for anyone else."

Izar smiled. "Yes, but we did, for I gave one to my new master in Durotrin."

"Well, using a similar process, Zef made a disc as big as a child's hand using a mould the shape of the sun. I have copied his idea, look, I have some here," he said, pointing at a corner of his bench.

"But how could these discs become a bowl?"

"Come look," said Yor as he dragged a heavy log, which was standing on one end, out from under his bench. The top of the log had a flat surface apart from in the middle where a round depression had been scraped out and smoothed. Yor picked up a disc and a deer antler that had been fashioned as a hammer.

"It takes great patience and care," he said as he held the disc in one hand with the edge of it over the depression in the log. He slowly rotated the disc as he tapped the edge with the hammer. Gradually, the disc started to curl at the edge as he relentlessly struck it. At first, the antler made untidy dents in the copper, but as he carefully turned it again and again, the dents began to join up. He stopped regularly, inverting the bowl and inspecting the underside.

"This is the point where great care must be taken, for if any of the dents are too deep the copper can crack."

When he was satisfied with the shaping of the bowl, he stopped using the depression in the log and started tapping his hammer with the metal now lying on the flat part of the log. Finally, the surface of the bowl was almost smooth.

Izar could contain himself no longer. "I must try to do this, for the bowl is an object of beauty, the like of which would bring me great respect in the land of the Duran."

This was the beginning of a period of many days when the two men worked together, experimenting and improving their skills. As well as knives, they cast arrowheads and, largest of all, a spearhead, which Izar carefully polished.

It was a few days before the traders arrived that Izar remembered that he had a surprise for Yor. He had brought with him one of the pieces of gnarled, dull, yellow metal the traders had given to his master. A present which the master had rejected.

"Yor, you will remember that on our long journey, I spoke to you of the possibility of other types of rock that might make metal of another kind."

"Yes, your imagination was often wild."

"I have another kind of metal, look at this."

Yor examined the ugly-shaped object.

"Where does this come from?" he asked.

"The land of the Silurians, a mountain people who live many days walk away from Durotrin, in the direction of the setting sun."

"It does have the texture of a metal, but not copper," said Yor.

"It seems to be heavier than our metal."

"How can it be used?" asked Yor.

"I don't know, it does not become a liquid in the hearth."

"Have you tried to heat it?"

"Yes, with no success."

They both continued to look at the misshapen lump and then, simultaneously at each other.

"Then we should try again," said Yor.

He gave the metal back to Izar and reached for his blow bag. He pumped the hearth a few times to get some life into the fire. Izar put the metal on the bench and picked up a basket of charcoal. He passed it to Yor.

"Put the lump in a clay dish, we will try to capture the metal if it melts."

Izar put the dish in the fire and, using a long bone, prodded it forward into the hottest part of the inferno.

A little while later, when the men judged that the fire had reached the right heat to melt copper, Izar used the bone to clear away some of the charcoal so they could better see the contents of the dish.

They both peered into the fire.

"See, it does nothing. It is still in the same form," said Izar.

They were both silent as they considered how the metal could be coaxed into changing its form. Then they both spoke at the same time, saying almost the same thing.

"The metal is heavier than copper, perhaps it needs more heat to melt," said Yor.

"This metal is of a different nature to copper. It may melt with more heat," said Izar.

Izar grabbed the blow bag and started to pump air into the glowing charcoal. The fuel crackled and sparks flew out dangerously from the inferno. The men leaned forward as close as they dared, peering at the dish, sweat now running down their faces. As they watched, the glowing metal suddenly began to disintegrate and form a pool in the container.

They had succeeded in melting gold.

CHAPTER 23

Once more Yor accompanied Izar and Radan to the ferry that would take them across the great sea. Their pack animal carried two baskets of raw copper, which they had traded with the men from the land in the direction of the midday sun.

"Yor, the gold is yours to keep, at Durotrin I have more pieces like the one I brought to you. I will use our new knowledge to make more of the metal and learn how to use it."

"And as we agreed, we can trade for as much copper as you need. If you get more pieces of the new metal, please send me some with the traders," answered Yor.

The task of loading the boats was complicated by the need to carry the donkeys. They hobbled them by tying the animals' legs together, and several men lifted them onto the craft, where they were lashed down.

Izar gave the boatmen a hunting dog to pay for their voyage. This was a trade that well satisfied the sailors, as the dogs from the land across the great sea were highly regarded.

When they arrived safely in the land of the Regni, their journey on land began. However, Izar now found himself more and more dependent on being able to ride the donkey.

Walking any distance brought on an increasingly dull ache in the leg that had been injured all those years ago.

Once more, the settlements they passed on their journey offered hospitality to the Duran warrior, the Rhetian and his dog. Though long, the journey was uneventful, and as they waited across the river from Durotrin for boats to carry them over, Izar was in high spirits. He was confident that the new knowledge he brought with him would boost his reputation and improve his prowess in the community. He was also looking forward to seeing Tan and he wondered how much the boy had grown.

"What's that noise?" asked Izar.

"It's the rumble of many people shouting, some distance away," answered Radan.

They both listened for a while. There was no doubt, it was the sound of a large crowd.

"Where are the fishermen? We need a boat to take us across," said Radan impatiently.

As he spoke, some people appeared from the settlement and they started running down the avenue to the river. The two men watched in horror as pursuers appeared behind those fleeing and started to fire arrows at them.

When the fugitives arrived at the water's edge, they started to push the boats drawn up on the riverbank into the water in an attempt to escape. The dog sensed his master's unease and barked loudly at those trying to cross the river. Fearing that it might attack them, Izar tied it to a sapling.

"Look, there are two of the men who were with us on the journey from the land of the Rhetians!" shouted Izar.

"Yes, and there are other men with them I know, they are good warriors," replied Radan.

Those who had managed to embark started to paddle furiously towards Radan and Izar. As they did so, their pursuers tried to stop them with arrows.

"Quick, string your bow, Izar, we must help them," said Radan as he pulled his out from under the pack on the donkey carrying their goods.

Izar did as instructed. As he pulled back the bow string, he trembled. He had suddenly remembered something that had happened a long time ago, the last time he had fired an arrow at a man. The memory was unpleasant, but now he had no choice but to help.

As the fleeing warriors reached the shore in front of them, Izar and Radan fired over their heads at the men on the other side of the river.

Men on the other bank made no effort to chase those escaping once they realised that they would be very vulnerable in a boat on the river.

"What is happening? Why are they chasing you?" Radan shouted to the men climbing out of the boats.

As he spoke, Izar noticed a pall of smoke rising from the village.

"We tried to protect the master, but we were too few," said a breathless man.

"But why? Who is attacking him?" demanded Radan.

"It is the work of the Wisemen. They use their mystical threats to frighten the people," he answered. "They have whipped everyone into a frenzy of hate and suspicion."

Izar stopped firing arrows and asked, "But what do they want? Look, some huts are burning! Why are they doing this?"

"They torched your hut, Radan," said one of the fugitives.

"Why is this happening? Did you see my woman and my boy?" said Radan.

"Yes, she ran to seek refuge in the forest with the Rhetians."

"And my boy too?" asked Izar.

"I think so, I expect he ran off with the others."

Izar glanced at Radan. His nostrils flared, his eyes narrowed and he clenched his teeth tightly. There was no mistaking his fury.

He looked round at the men and, pointing towards the edge of the river, growled. "Come, gather up the arrows they have fired at us, we might need them."

He walked down to the riverbank, oblivious to the danger of being targeted, and deliberately showed himself to the mob on the other side. The noise of the crowd diminished to silence, and then some arguments broke out among them before several left and started walking back to the village. Clearly, the appearance of the master's chief warrior had caused a number of the rioters to lose their nerve.

"Come, all of you. We'll walk down to where we can wade across the river and then we will deal with this insurrection," shouted Radan.

Izar untied the dog, he and Radan turned their donkeys and, together with the other men, hurried off on the track leading in the direction the river was flowing. Izar had mounted his donkey, for he otherwise had no chance of keeping up with the warriors.

As they walked, Radan took one of the men aside.

"Tell me, what has caused this violence?" he asked.

"Soon after you left, arguments started to break out about being forced to make changes to our way of life. The Wisemen kept telling the people that we have lived the way we do for more generations than we have hairs on our heads. They said that the Earth God gives us stone, good flint. We make our tools and weapons the way we always have. They said that the Rhetians were robbing the Earth God for something that is unnecessary. The land was being violated and we would all suffer terrible punishment unless we stopped it."

Another man interrupted, saying, "The master tried to defend the Rhetians, saying that the power they had to make things was a gift from the Earth God, and that our lives would be enriched by the fruit of the rocks. That Durotrin would become an even more important place and our tribe would be the greatest among all others."

"So, what has happened today?" asked Izar.

"The Wisemen told the people to defend their way of life and to kill the master."

"Kill him!" gasped Radan.

"Yes, we warriors tried to defend him, but it was impossible. The crowd was excited into madness by the language of the Wisemen."

"Is he dead?" asked a shocked Izar.

There was a silence. The men looked at each other uneasily.

"We saw him being dragged away to the ritual death place."

Izar remembered the altar stone in the centre of the circle of poles, a stone stained by the blood of the sacrifices.

"Surely they would not dare to murder him," gasped Izar.

"Yes, the Wisemen wanted it done before Radan returned to protect the master."

The group continued to hurry along the track until they came to the area almost opposite Izar's workshop, the place where the river split into several streams that could be forded. One of the men seized Izar's donkey's leading rope and pulled it into the water, following the others. On the other side, they started to climb the hill leading to the ritual killing place.

Unseen by them, a large crowd had gathered at the circle to witness the assassination of the master. The shouting had stopped and the only sound was the incantation of the Wisemen, but this was too faint for Radan and his followers to hear until they broke through the cover of the trees and out into the sunshine on the flat ground outside of the circle.

As the armed warriors walked around behind the crowd to reach the entrance, they were unseen by the people with their backs towards them. However, when they reached the entrance, the mob had full view of them, and the warriors had full view of the proceedings.

In the middle of the circle was the naked body of the old man, lying on his back on the altar stone. A stone dagger protruded from his chest. His left arm hung over the edge of the stone; it was red with the blood draining from his chest. The master's deer skull headdress lay on the grass in front of the altar.

The Wisemen noticed the annoying disturbance in the crowd and it directed their attention to the armed men by the entrance to the site.

People spectating moved around the poles to get a better view of the interlopers. The atmosphere was growing in intensity as they anticipated Radan's rage. They all knew, what Izar had never been told - the master was Radan's father.

"We are too late," lamented Radan. "I must take control of these men before they turn the crowd on us."

Radan's urge for vengeance was tempered by the wisdom he had inherited. He realised that his small band of warriors could not do more than threaten some of those nearest to them in this large crowd of people. He had to take over control of the mob from the Wisemen.

Izar felt a great urge to support his travelling companion. If the Wisemen could use their mystic powers to stir the crowd, then he would combat it with his own. He dismounted and walked back to the pack animal to collect something. Meanwhile, Radan handed his bow to one of the warriors and, unarmed, started to slowly walk along the narrow avenue to the centre of the circle.

The noise of the crowd subsided as they watched his progress. Everyone was waiting with growing anticipation to see what the late master's chief warrior would do. As he approached the Wisemen, three of their henchmen stepped forward to protect them from possible attack. Radan paid the men no heed as he reached the altar. In silence he regarded the body of his father. Then he turned and surveyed the crowd. He looked from one side to the other and then addressed them.

"The master is dead. He was the man who has made Durotrin prosperous. The man who made sure that you all had food to eat, that we could build great works to sanctify the gods who protect us. He was…"

Radan's speech was cut short by the three men, who at the behest of the Wisemen grabbed his arms and dragged him in front of them. They forced him to the ground.

The shirt of one of the Wisemen, the one wearing a bear's head headdress, was soaked in the blood of the man he had recently executed. He held one hand in the air and, as loudly as he could, shouted, "This is the man who seeks to help those who would bring change to our community! A man who seeks to destroy the ways of our fathers, and their fathers, and those beyond them. He must go the way of the master, his father!"

The crowd was clearly of differing views: some shouted encouragement to the speaker, others remained silent and glanced round nervously to see if they were in a minority.

The speaker stepped forward and drew the bloody knife out of the chest of the dead master. He stood before the crowd, waving the weapon in the air and shouted, "Like father, like son! This day, both will go from this world to the next!"

As he gradually lowered his hand, those nearest him heard a thud. The wiseman's headdress tumbled to the ground as he fell forward across the body of the master. The copper head of the arrow, which had pierced his throat, now protruded out the back of his neck as he fought to take his last breath.

Pandemonium broke out as all eyes turned to the group of warriors at the entrance of the circle. Izar put down his bow and picked up the long stave he used to support himself.

He set the dog free, took off its muzzle and let it walk beside him. To spectators, it seemed that his animal was his only protection. He slowly and painfully limped along the pathway towards the bloody scene at the altar. As he did so there were gasps of awe from the crowd. Some recoiled and others fell to their knees. Lashed at the top of his stave, shining brightly, reflecting the brilliance of the late afternoon sun, was a copper spearhead, a sight none of the watchers had ever seen before. Izar approached the centre of the circle and stood before the altar.

The men holding Radan released him and he stood up and held out his hand to the remaining Wiseman, beckoning him to hand over the dagger he had picked up from the ground. The intake of the crowd's breath was audible. Their faith in the belief that a Wiseman could only be killed by a god was already shaken. Was a second one also to be killed?

Radan held the dagger aloft and shouted, "You have been misled by the Wisemen! They believe that the knowledge the Rhetians have brought to us will threaten their power. This is not so. Yes, there will be changes as we learn to use the new materials, but these changes will bring more wealth and prowess to the Duran people and benefit all of you."

Pointing at the Wiseman beside him, he continued, "The killing of the master is avenged. But we still need Wisemen to plan our sacred sites. Such men have knowledge and understanding above that of others."

Pointing at the man beside him wearing the wolf's headdress, he said, "This Wiseman is spared to continue the work of glorifying our gods."

Picking up the discarded deer skull with the brightly coloured leather ribbons, he placed it on his head. He slowly surveyed the crowd in front of him and announced loudly, "You have a new master."

CHAPTER 24

For Radan and Izar, the euphoria of restoring order in Durotrin was soon overcome by anxiety regarding the whereabouts of their families and the Rhetians. The new master had the power to send out search parties in the forest to find his woman, his son and also Tan. The problem was that as soon as the searchers were seen by the fugitives, the frightened people would withdraw further into the sanctuary of the woods. It was therefore necessary for Izar to join those sent out to look for them. He could call out in the language of the Rhetians in the hope that they might hear him and get reassurance that it was safe for them to return. The forest was too dense for him to use his donkey and the strain on his leg from the walking slowly caused the dull ache to change to a pain he began to find intolerable.

It took two days before animal trackers using Izar's dog managed to trace the missing people. On his assurance they willingly returned to Durotrin. Radan's woman and his boy followed the group back into the village.

"Have you seen Tan?" Izar asked his landsmen as they walked back towards the settlement.

"No, he was not with us," said one.

"I last saw him with your woman. She didn't go with the rest of us," said another.

Thus, the hunt for Tan turned into a search for Fer, the woman who had been living with Izar and Tan, but she was nowhere to be found. People confirmed that she too had run away, frightened because of her association with a man despised by the Wisemen.

Despite his concern for his son, as the days and weeks passed, Izar forced himself into supervising the work needed to produce charcoal and begin to put into practice the lessons he and Yor had learned when they were recently together.

His hopes about Tan were raised when, at the beginning of the cold time, when the days were no longer than the nights, Radan arrived at his workshop accompanied by a dishevelled and weeping woman. It was Fer.

"Where did you find her?" asked Izar.

"I sent messengers out to the villages around here, men who would recognise her. She was living with another man in a small settlement a day's walk from here."

The woman stared at the ground, unresponsive to Izar.

"Where is he? Where is Tan?" demanded Izar.

She looked up, tears in her eyes. She sobbed as she said, "The Wisemen took him."

She paused, took a deep breath and continued, "They seized him. I tried to stop them, but they threatened me. They said I must leave Durotrin immediately."

Izar put his head in his hands. He sobbed as he said, "Oh no. Radan, you know what this means."

"Yes, we came back too late."

Izar uncovered his tortured face and shouted, "Too late to stop Rhetian blood flowing on the altar!"

There was a deep furrow on Radan's brow, a sign of both the pity and anger he felt, as he admitted, "Yes, I am afraid so."

"Go, go I must be alone to grieve."

"What do you want me to do with the woman?"

Izar looked at the wretched figure in front of him and said quietly, "Send her back to her new man. It was not her fault."

In the days and weeks that followed, Izar gradually came to terms with the terrible fate that had befallen his son. As grief subsided, his dedication to his work increased. Nevertheless, hardly a day passed when he did not climb up the hill to the ritual place and stand in front of the bloody altar in silence, thinking about the son he had lost. In truth there was little sign of the awful deeds that had taken place on the stone slab. The wind and rain of the cold time, which always seemed to come from the direction where the sun set in the dark time of the year, had all but washed the alter clean. While the weather could expunge the mark of the slaughter, nothing could eradicate Izar's regret that he had not insisted on taking the boy with him on his recent journey. Only immersion in his work could take his mind off the tragedy.

In the workshop, Izar had made great progress in shaping copper by the method Yor had shown him. Once he had perfected the skill of creating a regular shaped disc of the material, he and two of his Rhetian assistants began to create small bowls. Izar always did the finishing work using a light piece of antler and a cushion made of smoothed flint. He tapped the copper very gently against the cushion to create a smooth surface, which reflected the light of the fire in the hearth.

When he was satisfied that he could not improve the objects further, he took the two finest ones to show Radan.

Using his walking stave as support, he painfully limped through teeming rain to the village.

He stood at the doorway and called, "Greetings, Radan, the mud is thicker than ever. When will the rain stop?"

"It is good to hear you, Izar. We may have rain and wind, but surely that is better than the frost and snow of your old home."

"Perhaps. At least I can work all year here, not like in the Rhetian mountains."

Radan opened the leather curtain and the hurdle. He noticed that his visitor was carrying a leather bag.

"Have you something to show me? It has been a long time since we returned home with the copper. Come in, out of the rain."

They entered the hut and Izar sat on the ground while Radan settled on the log that once was his father's seat. A fire was blazing in the hearth.

Izar brushed the rain drops off the top of his bag and opened it.

"I have learned how to form copper so that it can make a useful shape."

Izar pulled out one of the bowls and handed it to Radan. He took and with reverence held it up to inspect it. Izar was gratified to see that the flames from the fire were mirrored on the outside of the bowl, the tint of the copper enriching the colour.

"This is a thing of great beauty, Izar," said Radan quietly. "Can you make more like it?"

The Rhetian pulled the second one from his bag and held it up.

"It is good that you have made these, for in a few days visitors will begin to arrive in Durotrin for the feast to celebrate the middle of the cold time, the time when the old year dies and the new one begins."

"So, news of the achievements of your people will be spread. Where will the visitors come from?"

"From far afield. There will be people from the lands of the Regni, the Belgae and Siluria, even the Taexali from the lands very far from here, they who travel with the midday sun on their faces. They will come to see the great works that we, the Durans have built. They must also be shown the miracles you create."

"Will the place of the dead be finished by then?"

"No, there is more work to be done on the outside. More of the great bocks of stone are needed. They can't be transported in the wet time of the year, but the digging of the holes continues."

"How will you show others, the visitors, what marvels are produced in my workshop?"

"We will make a covered place near to your workshop where your products can be inspected and sold."

"Sold?" said Izar with consternation.

"Yes, we will trade your work for things my people need: grain, animals, honey, and promises of allegiance to me. This way our people will see that we keep the promise that I made, that the changes we make will be to their favour."

"What if I use all the copper we traded from Yor?."

"We will trade more as we need it. I'll send men to do this. Now you must be quick and make more bowls like these, knives and even arrow and spear heads."

Izar felt a mixture of emotions: worry about Radan's demands and pride that his work had assumed such importance to his master.

The next weeks were ones of intensive activity in the workshop, while Izar and his assistants used such daylight as there was to produce knife blades and copies of the bowls he had shown Radan. The all-consuming nature of the work absorbed the metal worker as he strove to satisfy his master's demands. With his mind thus occupied in daytime, Izar had little time to dwell on the loss of his son, but when night fell, he became morose and lonely, feelings exacerbated by the ache in his leg. He reflected on the fact that his ambition to be the foremost metal worker in this, the far country, had cost the lives of his little friend Lin, his Rhetian woman, his son and he had even lost the Duran woman the master had given him. Nevertheless, he was now a man of high standing in the land of the Duran. He had more prestige than old Rab ever had. But Rab and Stin would be dead now; perhaps Nir was the new master in the village where Izar had learnt his trade. He found himself wondering about his father and mother, though he realised that they must surely have died some time ago. What became of his brother? He regretted that his family in the Rhetian mountains never learned of his success. Yes, he was successful and had prowess, but he could go further, he was not satisfied yet, he wanted to find new ways to improve the art of making and using metals, and he was gradually beginning to realise that his life would be always so. Contentment would always elude him.

The distance from the workshop to the village was such that Izar was not aware of the influx of strangers who had travelled long distances to attend the mid-winter rituals. There was one exception. Travellers coming from the direction where the winter sun set, walked along the track that passed his workshop. One day he was disturbed by the noise of many people talking excitedly and laughing raucously. Some were riding on small horses, a sight which Izar had seldom seen before. A few sat on horse-drawn carts stacked with trading goods, but most were walking. After they had passed, one of his assistants came in to tell him that he had heard they were Dumnonii people, a tribe with a bad reputation for thievery and murder.

In the village there were strangers from every part of the land, men, women and children. Some carried goods on their backs, others drove cattle or pigs ahead of them as they arrived. The things they carried and the beasts were to be given in exchange for hospitality and feasting, or to trade with.

News of the Duran metal working had spread through the different tribes and it was not long before Izar found himself the object of many visitors' interest. Reed screens had been put up around his workshop to stop prying eyes, but this did not stop some people trying to peer through the gaps to view the mystic spectacle of the proceedings within. Eventually, Radan had to provide guards to keep visitors at a distance. At the same time, builders were erecting a huge shelter nearby. When it was complete, they set up benches for the display of Izar's work. Soon after, Radan arrived to inspect the construction.

"Izar, the Wiseman has told us that tomorrow we will have the longest night and the shortest day. In the morning there will be a great procession to the Place of the Dead. The tribal leaders will take their people to see the great sight. Many visitors will walk on this track, past your workshop. When we return, I will show the tribal leaders your work and we will make trade. While we are at the ritual site you should put your best copper work on the benches for us to see."

"Now I have used all the copper we traded from Yor. We must get more."

"If we are successful tomorrow, you shall have more. Now I must return to the feast."

CHAPTER 25

It was as Radan said: in the morning there was a seemingly endless line of strangers trudging past the workshop, in an ever-increasing sea of mud, as the track was churned by many feet. When they returned, Radan introduced Izar to the tribal headmen, who then surveyed the articles on display. They in turn were watched by a vast crowd of people who stood jostling around the outside of the shelter.

Radan took Izar aside, his beaming face that of a happy man.

"Izar, we have done good trade!" he said.

"They liked the work?"

"Yes, all of the headmen wanted something to take back with them to show their people, that is all of them except one, the leader of the Dumnonii. He claims that he has a Wiseman who can make such articles."

"Is it possible?"

With some consternation on his face, Radan said, "It is difficult to know. He had nothing to show us."

Smiling once more, he said, "We got good payment for the copper. Next warm season, several of the tribes will bring us cattle and sheep. A few will bring grain."

"This pleases me, for your people will see that my work benefits them all."

"And your reputation will be even greater."

"As will yours, Radan."

When the headmen moved on to join the festivities in the village, Izar and his helpers cleared the few items that had not been traded and took them to the safety of the workshop. The Rhetians then set off to join the merry making, but Izar declined to join them.

Aware of the value of his copper work, Radan had some time ago insisted that a large wooden box should be placed underground in the workshop. It was installed in secret by Radan's most trusted servants and used for the safekeeping of the articles. The lid was hidden by a cowhide mat.

As soon as everyone had left, Izar lifted the mat and opened the lid. He placed the few remaining pieces of copperware into the box and took out a small leather package. He then replaced the lid and the mat.

Izar had no copper left to work with, but this gave him time to do something that had been on his mind ever since returning to Durotrin. He put the package on the bench and eagerly opened it. Inside was the remainder of the gnarled lumps of metal, the gift the old master had rejected and given to him.

Izar started to repeat the process he and Yor had followed to melt the gold. Before darkness had fallen, he had a small quantity of the gleaming metal cooling in a clay crucible. When the new metal had solidified and cooled, he broke the crucible and started to examine the material. His real hope was that it might be harder than copper so that he might make sharper, longer lasting blades. He was disappointed. As he tapped the circular lump with his antler hammer, the metal started to change shape, obeying the dictate of the pressure put upon it. The lump became thinner and thinner, while the flat, circular shape increased in width.

As Izar's disillusionment increased however, it was at first tempered and soon overwhelmed by the recognition of the sheer beauty of the shape in front of him. It shone in the lamplight with a radiance that surpassed even the most polished of his copperware.

The sound of the dog growling made him aware that some of his Rhetian helpers, who had huts nearby, were returning from the feast. He quickly moved the mat and hid the small plate of gold in the box. The growling got louder. Izar tied the dog to his bench and went to the door of the workshop to look outside. The people returning would have flaming torches to light their way, but there were none to be seen. Izar felt some unease and returned inside to get his bow, which was leaning on the work bench. He picked it up and quickly strung it. He took an arrow from the quiver hanging from the ceiling beam and placed it, ready to fire.

There was a loud crash as the hurdle covering the door opening was smashed in. By the light of his lantern, Izar could see a man holding in one hand a long flint knife; with the other, he pushed the broken parts of the hurdle out of the way to gain entry.

"Put the bow away and come with me," said the stranger.

The man spoke the Duran way, but his speech had an accent that told Izar he was one of the visitors to Durotrin.

"Stand back or I'll kill you," threatened Izar.

A voice behind the stranger shouted, "Get him. The cripple can't use a bow. He won't hit you."

A second man appeared behind the first.

Izar wondered, if he shot the first man, would the other run away?

There was a twang as Izar loosed the arrow. The man with the knife twisted sideways, howling as he slumped across a pile of charcoal. Izar grabbed another arrow, but the second stranger was too fast for him. He knocked the Rhetian off his feet and jumped on him, restraining him, as he lay on the ground. Two more men entered the workshop and helped to bind Izar's hands.

"Who are you? What do you want?" protested Izar.

"We are Dumnonii people. Our master wants you to do for him what you have done for Radan."

"No. I serve Radan, my master."

"You have a new master now," said one of the men, laughing as he spoke.

Izar was dragged outside and bundled onto a cart, which had just arrived. Judging by the sound of voices, there was a large group of people approaching from the village.

"Here come the other Dumnonii, we will all travel together to our territory."

Izar looked round and realised that the approaching crowd was increasingly illuminated by light from the workshop. The two men inside had set fire to the structure.

They came out and one remarked, "There will be no more copper produced here."

"But my dog! It's inside."

The men laughed and one shouted, "Let's go."

The cart jerked into motion as the horse took the strain and tried to get a grip on the muddy track. Izar repeated his desperate plea for the dog, but to no avail. Very quickly, the flames had engulfed his workshop and his hut. He was on his way to the land of the Dumnonii.

It was later, much later, that the Rhetians returned from the feast. Their huts were some way from the workshop and although several of them noticed a smell of smoke, the fire had burned out and there were no longer any flames to indicate to them that there was anything amiss. It was in the morning when they rose that the catastrophe was detected.

Radan was summoned and after the debris was cleared, he declared solemnly that the severely burnt, unrecognizable body they found was that of his friend, Izar. His dog had also been a victim of the fire. No doubt, the pioneer metal smith had had an accident with the metal working hearth, which had caused the building and his charcoal store to catch fire. Radan grieved for Izar, but he was equally concerned about the effect that the Rhetian's death would have on the prowess of the Duran.

The master announced, "Izar was a great man, the foremost and cleverest metal smith in the known world. His body has been purified by fire. His bones will be buried in a pit in the Place of the Dead." The Rhetian settlers protested that the body should be laid in a grave, in the manner of their custom, but Radan's will prevailed.

That Radan had his way meant that elaborate ritual would take place among the massive stones at the now nearly completed site. Three days later the funeral procession, led by the Wiseman and Radan, wended its way from the village past the burnt-out site of Izar's workshop towards the Place of Death. The bones of the deceased had been disassembled and cleaned. They were in a heap in a wicker basket carried by the Rhetians. The mid-winter wind whipped across the open landscape to the discomfort of those negotiating the muddy track. That the area was almost treeless lent drama to the view of the stark, white pillars of stone when they came into view. Neither was the drama diminished as the procession approached the site, for the aura generated by wonderment at the sheer size of the monoliths imbued reverence in the spectators, and the chattering of the walkers ceased. The villagers formed a circle on the outside of the stones; only the Wiseman and Radan and those carrying the wicker basket entered the circle. The basket was set on the altar and the Wiseman began his incantation. Radan placed a boar's tusk in the basket to signify courage, determination and power.

The wildness of the weather added to the austere atmosphere and as if on cue, no sooner had the Wiseman finished his chant, than the rain came. The increasing severity of the storm seemed to underscore the frailty of the people gathered and contrasted it with the solidity of the structure in front of them. The ritual being over, the basket was taken outside of the stones to the edge of the great ditch. There, a group of boys, the waifs who dug the holes on the site, stood, inadequately dressed for the weather. The pit they had just finished was to be the last resting place for the man's mortal remains.

As the bones were being placed into the ground, the rain intensified further. Yet the urchins still stood watching, intrigued by the sight of the bones. The downpour washed the chalk from their hair and faces. As Radan glanced at them, he received his second shock in three days. One of the boys was different from the others: he had fair hair and blue eyes.

"Is it possible? It is you, Tan, surely? Yes, it must be you!" shouted Radan against the howl of the wind and the hiss of the rain.

"Yes, Master, I was Tan, but they made me change my name so that no one would know me."

"Who did?"

"When the Wisemen took me for sacrifice, they saw from the marks on my hands that I was too old to be sacrificed on the altar."

Radan turned to the Wiseman. "Is this so? Did you seek to punish this boy because you hated his father?"

"Master, it is no punishment to be sacrificed to the Earth God, but a privilege."

"And when you found that he was too old, he was placed here with the other slaves?"

"Here too it is an honour to serve the gods."

Radan looked down at the bones in the pit and reflected, wondering if the boy realised whose they were. He looked up at the ragged figure in front of him and said, "Come, boy, you will come back to the village with me. I will care for you."

CHAPTER 26

Izar's fury over being seized from his home and the loss of his dog hardly abated as the journey progressed. At first, he feared that the men around him might treat him badly, for they had showed no mercy when they dragged him from his workshop. But after the first day, his hands were untied and he travelled reasonably comfortably on the back of the cart as a passenger, albeit an unwilling one. The vehicle had large, solid wooden wheels that jolted on the slightest unevenness on the track. Though he was frequently shaken and often had to grab the side of the cart to avoid being thrown off, his lot was easier than that of those walking ahead of him.

His captors were rough, barbaric men who showed him none of the respect he was used to getting in Durotrin. However, it was clear that they had been instructed to keep him well fed and alive. The column of travellers was led by their master and his closest men, all of whom were riding on horseback. They skilfully controlled the small, brown horses by means of leather lines attached to a piece of wood in the back of the horse's mouth. Izar had never seen such an arrangement before; indeed he had only on a few occasions seen horses being ridden. He noted that these animals were much more willing than donkeys and also much faster. Each rider had an animal skin they sat on and a pack of belongings tied on the back of the horse with a rope that went under and around the animal's belly.

The cart was at the end of the long line of travellers and one horseman rode alongside it, seemingly to ensure that the captive did not jump off and escape. In reality this could not happen as Izar was restricted by his physical capability. This lone horseman had no conversation apart from when Izar very occasionally asked him about the horse or his riding skills. The Rhetian was mainly left alone with his thoughts. These were dominated by his recent experience with the gold. He was excited about the possibilities that the metal offered. However, his enthusiasm was much dampened by the realisation that in his new situation, he was unlikely ever to have a chance to continue with this work.

Each afternoon, as soon as the daylight faded, the travellers pitched simple tents in which they spent the nights. Cooking fires were lit and Izar was helped down to join the others and eat with them. He had no tent, so he slept under the cart on a bed of leaves he scraped together from the forest edge. Despite the time of year, the weather was mild and dry. It was on the morning of the third day that things changed. As the people packed their tents and made ready to leave, the wind became noticeable. At first the boughs of the mighty beech trees on both sides of the track gracefully swayed as the breeze blew in the direction they were travelling. With the wind on their backs, they set off. However, Izar was particularly exposed as he sat facing backwards. He took the cowhide on which he had been sitting and huddled behind it, for he was still wearing the indoor clothes he had on when he was captured.

Grey clouds scudded across the sky, adding to the darkness of the deep forest in which they were making their way forward. The storm that had disrupted the ceremony at the Place of the Dead had reached them. The wind started to gust more strongly. Wet leaves that normally would have remained firmly on the ground started to overtake the cart and make the horses skittish. The loud rattle of the branches above them as they waved and weaved in the wind added to the cacophony. But this force of nature was pushing people, animals and the carts in the right direction, so there was no great hardship, that is until, quite suddenly, the first rain squall hit the convoy. There were voices of protest from the walkers as many asked to stop to shelter in the forest along one of the side paths crossing the track they were on, but the riders at the head of the column paid no heed. Now the squalls became even more frequent so that the extreme force of the gusts was almost continuous. The noise was now demonic as the wind swept through the trees and howled as if some monster was expressing anger at the travellers.

Izar heard a loud crack followed by screams further ahead. The cart stopped. He heard the driver shout to the horse rider. The latter dismounted, tied his horse to the back of the cart and ran forward. Izar craned round to see what had happened. Further on, a large branch of a beech tree had fallen in front of some of the walkers. The dismounted rider and the cart driver were running to help remove it. As Izar watched, several other branches came crashing down between the cart he was on and those trying to remove the entanglement of the first branch.

The horse that had been tethered to the cart had turned to face into the wind and was now trying to find cover alongside where Izar sat. He forced himself up, struggling against the power of the tempest and leaned over to grab the horse's mane with one hand while he untied the animal with the other. It stood still as the wind blasted it, though clearly it was jittery.

Izar put his leg over the rider's pack and gently mounted the horse. He grabbed the lines connected to the wood in its mouth. The horse responded, though hesitantly, as Izar gently kicked his heels into its flanks. It started walking slowly forward into the full force of the wind and the stinging rain. The Rhetian was hugely excited and nervous as he left the cart behind him. He realised that he had to get off the main track as soon as he could, for when his disappearance was discovered, the other riders, who were far more proficient than he was, would soon overtake him.

To the relief of horse and rider, they were soon able turn off into what was no more than a footpath, leading off the main track. The shelter afforded by the alder, bramble and hazel growing between the great beeches gave some refuge from the wind. However, that Izar sat high up on horseback, and that the overhead canopy of the forest reduced the footpath almost to a tunnel, meant that he had to duck under branches and frequently detach the tags of climbing bramble. They slowly continued on into the forest. The dense woods gave good cover despite the obstacles it presented. Anyone following would not be able to move faster than he could. Would they be able to see his tracks? He glanced behind him to see if the horse was leaving easily identifiable hoof prints that would betray his route and was relieved to see that the wind was creating swirls of leaves that covered the ground behind them. Nevertheless, when the expert Dumnonii horsemen could not find him on the track, they would surely search the forest paths. He must move on as fast as he could, though he knew the trail was not leading him back to Durotrin.

As the initial excitement of his escape decreased, he became more and more aware that he was very wet and suffering increasingly from the cold. He had no warm clothing, neither did he have food or any means of defending himself if he met a bear or wolves. He judged that had he been able to see the sun, it would now be at its highest point of the day, so he had some daylight left before he had to decide how and where to spend the night.

Some time later, he came to a stream and allowed the horse to drink. The Rhetian watched as the animal drank deeply. The rain had stopped, and the wind was dropping. Izar was tired and hungry. He was tempted to get off and drink himself, but he was aware that once he was on the ground it might be difficult for him to remount. Having satisfied its thirst, the animal stood motionless waiting for an indication from the rider as to what it should do. No indication came, for Izar was dozing.

Eventually the horse gave a shrug. The rider was jolted into consciousness. He realised that he was just too tired continue. Hunger and the exertion of the ride had taken its toll. He held on to the horse's mane and twisted to slide off. As he did so his weak leg was obstructed by the pack strapped on behind him. He had forgotten all about it! With the horse tied to a sapling, he opened the pack. The cover was the rider's bed fur. Inside was a leather package containing bread and pig's meat, clearly saved from the feast, together with a flint knife and some arrow heads.

Izar noticed the horse tossing its head up, sniffing. It had detected a smell that was as yet too weak for a human to notice. Were they being followed? Izar quickly repacked the fur and tied it back on the horse. He tried several times to remount. Years of wielding a hammer in his work shops had given him a very strong upper body, and eventually he managed to pull himself up onto the patient animal. He sniffed; he too could smell it – wood smoke! Behind him were perhaps men hunting him and in front there must be a dwelling. The choice was obvious: he kicked the horse and resumed his ride.

As he walked into the clearing, he realised that the old man was more observant than he was, for the wolfskin-clad person in front of him was already prepared to meet a stranger. He had his bow drawn and an arrow pointed directly at Izar.

"Who are you?" growled the wizened man.

"I am Izar, a hungry traveller."

"What brings you here? Stay still, don't come closer," he commanded.

"Fear."

"Fear of what?"

"I am being hunted. I am a great man in Durotrin, and enemies seized me."

"What enemies?"

"Men of the Dumnonii tribe."

The old man cleared his throat and spat on the ground before saying, "Thieves and murderers."

Izar looked around the clearing. There were two simple huts, one larger than the other. The smaller hut had obviously been damaged in the storm. While he was surveying the scene, the man stepped forward, showing an interest in the horse while still pointing the arrow at the rider.

"I can prove that I come as a friend, I have food," said Izar. "Let me get down and I will show you."

Izar had rightly surmised that at this time of the year, food would be very scarce for someone who had the appearance of living on hunting. Very soon, the two of them were sitting on a log in front of a fire in the larger hut, sharing the meat. There was more than enough for the two of them so Izar repacked the meat and put it back on the horse. The animal itself was grazing on such grass as there was around the edges of the clearing. The interior of the hut was very dark, but in its simplicity and design it reminded Izar of a hut he had once lived in - that of Old Rab.

"It'll soon be dark, help me repair the wall on the other hut," demanded the old man coarsely.

They went outside and Izar realised that he had not tethered the horse. He did so and then joined the man, who was standing by a pile of freshly cut young saplings. Clearly, he must have been busy cutting them when he became aware of an intruder. Together they stood the branches against the hole in the wall and wove twisted foliage through the saplings to hold them in place. By the time they had finished, it was almost dark.

"If you want to stay here tonight you can sleep in there," said the old man, pointing at the repaired hut.

"I would like that," replied Izar. He considered that the food he had shared and the work he had done was just payment for the lodging. What he had not noticed was that the hut was used for the treatment of animal pelts. There were several skins stretched out on wooden frames and the pungent smell of the scrapings underneath them pervaded the air. Stumbling about in the dark, Izar cleared a space large enough for him to wrap the fur round himself and sleep.

Despite his tiredness, sleep was fitful and nervous. Before first light he was dozing when he heard noises outside. He knelt up and peeped through a gap in the wall. To his horror he saw that the old man was standing with a spear, aiming it at the horse. He was trying to find a good angle to impale the weapon in the animal. The horse seemed to sense the danger and was weaving and twisting while tugging at its tether.

Izar leaped to his feet and limped out, barefoot, as fast as he could to intervene.

"What are you doing!" he shouted.

The man continued trying to find an opportunity to throw the spear accurately.

"You brought me more than one meal when you rode this animal here!" the man replied.

Izar launched himself at the old man and seized his shoulder just as he threw the spear. It flew harmlessly into the forest, just missing the horse's back. The force of Izar colliding with the man sent them both crashing to the ground. Despite his apparent age, his adversary was very strong, and it took a huge effort for Izar to prise the man's hands from his throat.

The pair of them rolled around on the wet grass, trading punches and kicks until age told and the old man stretched out on his back, gasping for air. Izar dragged himself to his knees and slowly stood up. He wiped his sleeve across his face to mop the blood flowing from his nose and the scratches on his face while looking disdainfully at the wretched figure moaning on the ground. Leaving the man where he was, he went back to the hut where he had slept. He strapped on his leather foot covers and gathered up his bed fur before walking over to the horse and remaking the pack. The old man was now sitting on the ground with his back against his hut. Not far from him his bow and quiver were propped up against the wall. Izar realised there was a danger that the man might try to stop him as he left. He walked across, grabbed the arrows out of the quiver and threw them as far as he could into the forest.

CHAPTER 27

When he approached the place where the footpath joined the track where he had made his escape the day before, Izar stopped the horse and listened intently. There was no sound apart from bird song. He kicked the horse's flanks, joined the trail, and turned the animal's head towards Durotrin. His journey was uneventful and the only person he met was a trader. Izar had swapped the arrow heads he found in the pack on the horse for dried meat and bread.

After three days, at around midday, he came out of the forest into a wide-open landscape. In the far distance he could see the white shape of the stones and he knew that he was almost home. As he passed the Place of the Dead, he saw the boys digging in the middle of the circle and he noticed that by the ditch, in the grass, there was a patch of brown earth, flecked with small, white pieces of chalk. The sign of a recent burial.

When he came to the site of his workshop, he saw the full horror of the fire damage. Rain had darkened the grey ash. Here and there were several half-burnt beams, the fire not having fully consumed the heavy oak frame of the building. He dismounted and tethered the horse.

After some time spent dislodging charred timbers, Izar found what he was looking for. The cowhide mat was badly singed, but the lid it was protecting was intact. Kneeling in the ashes, Izar pulled at the wood and removed it. He reached inside and felt around for the smooth disc. When he pulled out the small gold plate, it gleamed in the light of day, though there was no sun to truly do it justice. He replaced the lid and walked back to the horse. As he clambered onto its back, he noticed how filthy he was. His leather shirt and leggings were streaked with black marks from the timbers, his hands were coloured likewise and had he been able to see it, his face too. He set off for the village on horseback, holding up the shining disc for all to see.

Izar had expected that the people he passed who knew of him, and most did, would be surprised to see him return, but he had not expected the reaction he received. Some just looked, open mouthed as if astounded, others screamed, and some ran away. As he rode through the causeway into the village and onto the pathway through the great poles, men stopped work to gaze with astonishment. There was a loud babble of voices as the village folk expressed their wonderment.

The noise outside of his hut disturbed the master, it being redolent of the roar of the crowd on that day when his father was killed. He left his food and went out to find the source of the commotion.

Radan was an experienced warrior and now, statesman. Even he found it difficult to retain his composure at the sight of the metal smith who had arisen from the ashes and now confronted him. After his initial shock, he beckoned Izar to come into his hut. One of his men took hold of the horse's tether and Izar dismounted.

"I have something for you, Radan," said Izar, holding up the small disc. "This is the metal that will make your village truly famous."

Radan looked at the gold and smiled.

"Come in, we must talk."

He sent his servant out of the house and Izar told his tale in private. The master also had a story to tell, that of a ritual burial. But he missed out one important fact. At length, Radan said, "I would indeed look foolish if it were known that the bones we have buried were those of a Dumnonii villain. I think it best that we share this secret. It will not harm your reputation or mine that here in Durotrin we have a metal smith who can truly work miracles."

"I will need a new workshop."

"You will have all you need. But come now, I have a miracle to show you."

Outside the hut Radan took the spear that his guard was holding and gave it to Izar.

"Take this for support, we are going to visit a house in the village. I want you to meet someone."

At the time Izar found his way back to Durotrin after the Dumnonii had tried to force him to work for them, most of his life had gone for he had three rows of dots on one hand, two full rows and three single dots on the other. If he was lucky, he might eventually have four full rows of dots, but he was not destined to be so fortunate. The pain in his injured leg was now constant and, because he had always put his weight on the other one, the knee in his good leg was worn out and this pained him too. Nevertheless, he continued to work, trying to perfect the shaping of copper articles. But his real passion was exploring the properties of the new material, gold. He learned to beat the metal into small, thin sheets from which he produced the most expensive things he ever made in his career – shining, gold bindings to hold the hair tresses of wealthy men and women. Few could afford these objects, but they were much sought after by those who could.

The metal smith was never to meet his friend Yor again, but from time to time when the Duran traders went across the great sea to trade with him for copper, Izar sent one or two gold nuggets. However, they were increasingly difficult to obtain from the Silurian traders, who told that the material was now being sought in underground holes. They told other tales too about how Silurian metal smiths were blending other materials with copper to make it harder. The future for metal smithing was exciting and, to Izar's delight, Tan showed an avid interest in learning from his famous father.

Something else that pleased the Rhetian was that news of his success and that of the others who had made that long journey with him, had filtered back to the land of his birth. This had prompted more to make the long trek to cross the great sea. Their increasing numbers in the land of the Duran strengthened the possibility of acceptance and adoption of their ways and customs.

By the time Izar had three rows of dots on each hand and four more, toothache added to his physical discomfort.

As the pain became more and more unbearable, the infection from his tooth spread first to his throat and then gave him a constant headache. When Tan found him cold on the floor of the workshop, the boy's grief was shared by the whole Durotrin community, led by Radan. This time the master agreed to allow the Rhetians to bury the metal smith according to their tradition and return his body to the Earth God. They decided that his grave should be near to his workshop.

Izar was buried in a wood-lined grave. Following the custom in the land of his birth, he was laid on his side, with his knees bent, facing the direction from where, in the time of short days and long nights, the bitterly cold winds blew. The Rhetian community put in the grave the things he would need in the spirit world. There they placed beakers, boar tusks, his bow and arrows as well as the finest of arrowheads. Some of his metal working equipment was included too so that he could carry on his work. And as proof to the gods of the dead man's competence, Tan placed three of his father's copper knives next to him. Finally, in an act to demonstrate his gratefulness to the man who had once saved his life and had been instrumental in building the reputation of Durotrin, Radan took the two gold bindings from his own hair and placed them in the grave.

The End

EPILOGUE

BACKGROUND TO THE STORY

In May 2002 staff from Wessex Archaeology were concluding the examination of a proposed site for a new school in Amesbury, Wiltshire, just two miles from Stonehenge and near to the prehistoric settlement of Durrington Walls. They had found some Roman remains and decided to investigate a hollow area in the ground before closing the search. What they found there was the grave of a man buried around 2,300 BC. It was the richest early Bronze Age burial ever found in the Britain. Among the almost one hundred items in the grave were the oldest datable gold objects ever discovered in the country.

The skeleton in the grave was that of a man of between thirty five and forty five years of age. Examination of the bones gave some fascinating insights into the man's life:

His left leg was thinner than the right. It lacked a kneecap, the result of an injury. This would have caused the man to have a permanent and distinct limp and ultimately arthritic pain.

He had a hole through his jawbone, the result of a serious tooth abscess. This would have been very painful and the infection from the abscess could well have ultimately caused his death.

Oxygen isotope analysis of the man's teeth showed that he had been born and grew up in the region of the Alps, probably in the south of what is today Switzerland.

He had an unusual genetic abnormality of the instep of his foot. This was a very important clue to the identity of the body of a second man who was found in a nearby, later grave. There were golden hair tresses in his grave too. This man also had the genetic abnormality. They must have been related.

Items in the grave

- Three copper knives
- Two small, gold hair bindings
- A cushion stone used for metal working
- Two sandstone wrist guards to protect his wrists from the bow string
- Sixteen barbed and tanged flint arrowheads
- A bone pin, which would have been used to hold a piece of clothing such as a leather cloak
- Five Beaker pots
- A red deer spatula used for working flints
- Four boars' tusks
- Many flint tools and flakes

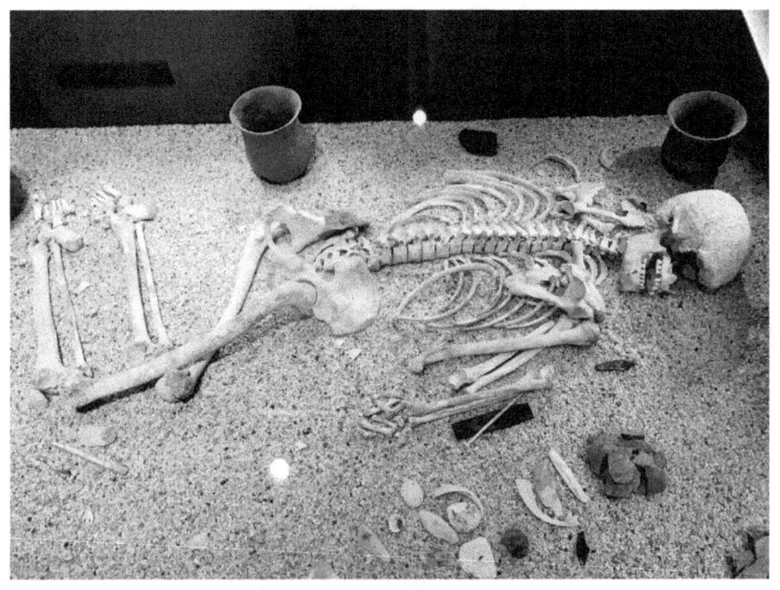

**A reconstruction of the burial, created
in Salisbury Museum.**

The various grave goods are shown in the position they were found in relation to the skeleton. The hole in the man's jawbone is seen clearly. While there is a knee cap by the right leg, there is none by the left one.

The gold hair tress binders

Reproduced by kind permission of Wessex Archaeology.

ACKNOWLEDGEMENTS

Thanks are due to Wessex Archaeology for the use of research material, and the expert advice of their Principal Osteologist, Jacqueline McKinley, who originally reported on the excavation of the Amesbury Archer's grave. Thanks too, to the metal smith at Butser Farm Ancient Village, for answering my interminable questions and showing me the copper melting process. I am grateful to my editor, Lisl Scully, for her incredible attention to detail and contributing useful ideas. My grandson, Oliver Thatcher, showed very helpful perception and depth of thought which belied his age, when acting as a beta reader.

As ever, I must express my gratitude to Barbro, my wife, for her encouragement and for her patient proof reading.

MEW

ABOUT THE AUTHOR

ichael E Wills was born on the Isle of Wight, UK, and educated at Carisbrooke Grammar and St Peter's College, Birmingham. After a long career in education, as a teacher, a teacher trainer and textbook writer, in retirement he took up writing historical novels. His first book, *Finn's Fate*, was followed by a sequel novel, *Three Kings – One Throne*. In 2015, he started on a quartet of Viking stories for young readers called, Children of the Chieftain. The first book, *Betrayed*, was described by the Historical Novel Society reviewer as "An absolutely excellent novel which I could not put down" and long-listed for the Historical Novel Society 2016 Indie Prize. The second book in the quartet, *Banished*, was published in December 2015 followed in 2017 by the third book, *Bounty*. *Bound For Home* completed the series in 2019. His book for younger children, Sven and the Purse of Silver, won bronze medal in the Wishing Shelf Book Awards.

Though a lot of his spare time is spent with grandchildren, he also has a wide range of interests including researching for future books, writing, playing the guitar, carpentry and electronics.

You can find out more about Michael E Wills and the books he has written by visiting his website: www.michaelwills.eu